THE SCARECROW

THE SCARECROW

IBRAHIM AL-KONI

TRANSLATED AND INTRODUCED
BY WILLIAM M. HUTCHINS

CENTER FOR MIDDLE EASTERN STUDIES
THE UNIVERSITY OF TEXAS AT AUSTIN

Cover image provided courtesy of the artist, Hawad.
Copyediting, cover and text design: Kristi Shuey
Series Editor: Wendy E. Moore

Library of Congress Control Number: 2015939478
ISBN: 978-1-4773-0252-1
Printed in the United States of America
Published in Arabic as *al-Fazza'a* (Beirut: al-Mu'assasa
al-'Arabiya li-l-Dirasat wa-l-Nashr, 1998).

The final section, "The Sacrificial Offering," appeared in
July 2011 as "The Sacrifice" on the website InTranslation at
brooklynrail.org.

TABLE of CONTENTS

CHARACTERS

Abanaban: chief vassal

Aggulli (or Aghulli): a sage and leader, recently assassinated

Ah'llum (or Ahallum): the hero, the tribe's head warrior

Amasis the Younger: a noble elder

Asaruf: a noble elder

Asen'fru: tax administrator

Chief Merchant: the man with two veils, de facto head
of the chamber of commerce

Emmamma: the tribe's venerable elder, a nobleman,
and the oldest man in the tribe

Imaswan Wandarran: spokesman for the Council of Nobles

Itinerant Diviner: handsome, black diviner with special gifts

Leader: a deceased poet compelled by Tuareg culture and his tribal
elders to lead a Tuareg tribe

Master of the Sign: African sage consulted by the sorcerer

Scarecrow (sorcerer, leader, strategist, governor, and various other
epithets): an inhabitant of the Spirit World who becomes
the ruler of the New Waw Oasis; Wantahet or his avatar

Tayetti: commander of the anti-gold campaign in *The Puppet*

Tomb Maiden or Priestess:
the deceased leader's bride and medium

INTRODUCTION

AL-KONI'S DEMONS

> Every so often out of the welter of the season's
> publications comes a book that is not an imitation of
> some other book. It has the touch of reality, the voice of
> a person; it spreads out a landscape of its own in which
> one moves with easy familiarity. One does not think of
> it as a book, but as a real world of comfortable unreality.

Hughes Mearns wrote this in his introduction for a selection of poems by
Edna St. Vincent Millay, not for a novel by Ibrahim al-Koni, although it
applies equally well to *The Scarecrow*. It seems uncanny that later, on the
same page, he continued:

> One might remark that a famous historic gentleman
> was an outstanding special pleader, a great soldier
> whose one defeat has amounted to an amazing victory,
> a distinguished actor of parts, a governor of a greater
> domain than that of any single nation of the present
> world, and guess as one might, no clue would be given
> to help in identifying the celebrated character. Few
> would know surely that the reference is to Beelzebub.[1]

What is uncanny here is that the main character of *The Scarecrow*
actually is a self-righteous, demonic despot who is as hollow as his physical
avatar—a scarecrow in the fields of the oasis.

The Scarecrow begins right where *The Puppet*, the preceding novel of
the New Waw or Oasis trilogy, left off. The conspirators, who assassinated
the last leader of this Saharan oasis community because he opposed the

---

1. Hughes Mearns, introduction to *Edna St. Vincent Millay*, by Edna St. Vincent Millay
(New York: Simon & Schuster, 1927), 8.

use of gold in business transactions, meet to choose his successor. The choice is complicated by metaphysical considerations. Two realms—al-khafa', the Spirit World, and al-khala', the desert wasteland and by extension the material world of everyday life—coexist in the same time and space, but people in the physical world are normally oblivious to the Spirit World, which unbeknownst to them controls them in many ways, most directly by "possessing" leaders the moment they mount the throne.

In an essay called "Is Life Worth Living?" William James told the story of a frisky terrier that bites a boy and then watches as the owner pays the boy's father, without having a clue as to its own involvement in this transaction.[2] James explained: "In the dog's life we see the world invisible to him because we live in both worlds."[3] He suggested that if we assume there is a bigger picture, a spiritual framework, we will find that our daily life is worth living, even though we are no more aware of the spiritual world than our feisty terrier is of our financial transactions concerning him. Here is an American version of the possible relationship between al-khafa', where the jinn (who rank between angels and human beings) live, and al-khala', where people live. James, in a different essay, explained that the gap between human and canine perspectives cuts both ways:

> Take our dogs and ourselves . . . how insensible, each of us [is], to all that makes life significant for the other . . . we to the rapture of bones under hedges, or smells of trees and lamp-posts, they to the delights of literature and art.[4]

A question for readers of Ibrahim al-Koni's works is whether the gap between human and jinn worlds challenges both us and the jinn who try to understand us. The Scarecrow suggests that the jinn may really lose their bearings when they visit our world.

---

2. William James, The Will to Believe and Other Essays in Popular Philosophy (Cambridge, MA: Harvard University Press, 1979), 52.
3. Ibid., 53.
4. William James, "On a Certain Blindness in Human Beings," in Essays on Faith and Morals, selected by Ralph Barton Perry (Cleveland, OH: The World Publishing Company, Meridian Books, 1962), 260.

In the novels of Ibrahim al-Koni, the dividing line between human beings and the jinn is blurred at times. In fact, wayfarers who meet in al-Koni's desert typically ask one another whether they are of jinni or human heritage.[5] In addition to leaders, other human beings who peep across the divide are diviners (like the tomb maiden in this trilogy), poets (often female in Tuareg culture), and Sufi dervishes. Not all jinn are demons, but all demons are jinn—or so it seems. Most of al-Koni's demonic characters are male, although the Mute Soprano at the beginning of *The Puppet* comports herself in a demonic manner;[6] most also serve as avatars—to some degree—of the Tuareg trickster Wantahet.

How coherent, then, are Ibrahim al-Koni's depictions of demons or the demonic through his many novels? Are all these demonic figures a single demon, several different demons, mere plot devices, or especially endowed characters? If there is one archdemon—say Wantahet of Tuareg mythology—is he more like Satan of the Abrahamic religions, Seth of ancient Egypt, or a West African trickster deity like Eshu? Put another way: since al-Koni identifies himself as a Saharan author, does it help to check out his neighborhood (Egypt to the east and West Africa to the southwest) and his own Sufi and European, etc., formation when interpreting his novels? Does comparison with Egyptian and African trickster gods illuminate al-Koni's depictions of the demonic?[7]

Luc-Willy Deheuvels, for one, has written that al-Koni's ideal reader will know everything about Arab and Islamic culture, Tuareg culture, and black African culture—not to mention European culture from ancient Greece to the present.[8] Ibrahim al-Koni himself has clearly stated that he views ancient Egyptian culture to be part of his Tuareg heritage. Some ancient peoples settled in the Nile Valley and others returned to the desert.[9]

---

5. See *The Seven Veils of Seth*, trans. William M. Hutchins (Reading, UK: Garnet Publishing, 2008), 134.

6. See *The Puppet*, trans. William M. Hutchins (Austin: Center for Middle Eastern Studies, at the University of Texas at Austin, 2010), 1–9.

7. Elliott Colla provides a cautionary tale in an article in *Banipal*; he was thinking of Jahili Arabic poetry in conjunction with a passage by al-Koni, who pointed him to *Moby-Dick* instead. Elliott Colla, "Translating Ibrahim al-Koni," *Banipal* 40 (Spring 2011): 175.

8. Luc-Willy Deheuvels, "Le lieu de l'utopie dans l'oeuvre d'Ibrahim al-Kawni," in *La Poétique de l'espace dans la littérature arabe moderne*, ed. Boutros Hallaq, Robin Ostle, and Stefan Wild (Paris: Presses Sorbonne Nouvelle, 2002), 25.

9. Ibrahim al-Koni, "Le 'discours' du desert: Témoinage," in *La Poétique de l'espace*, 97–98.

The protagonist of Ibrahim al-Koni's novel *al-Bahth 'An al-Makan al-Da'i'* (published in English as *The Seven Veils of Seth*) is a Satanic trickster named Isan who eventually destroys the oasis that has offered him its hospitality, but only because he wishes a better, destabilizing, nomadic existence for its residents. That novel's Arabic title is a play on Proust's famous title *A la recherche du temps perdu*; in al-Koni's novel the search is for lost space, for the lost paradise of Waw,[10] for which this new oasis, New Waw, has been named. The author encourages the reader to think of Isan as an avatar of Seth, who in the ancient Egyptian religion killed his brother Osiris (the good god of agriculture) in order to seize the throne, but who was also the desert god and therefore a benevolent champion of desert dwellers.

David S. Noss says that in ancient Iran, "The wild nomads to the north . . . were the scourge of all good settlers," and that their religion was a foil against which Zoroaster rebelled in founding Zoroastrianism as a religion for settled peoples and in transforming the nomads' godly devas into nature demons.[11] In *The Seven Veils of Seth*, Ibrahim al-Koni draws on the tension between these two opposing visions of Seth to provide depth to his portrait of his protagonist. Seth (or Isan), then, is not merely a demon but a god of necessary disorder.

The twentieth-century Iranian engineer, lay theologian, and reform politician Mehdi Bazargan explained in an essay: "Conflict, one of whose quintessential representatives for human beings is Satan, is the cause of a plethora of blessed events, from the natural cycle of life on earth to the higher cycle of resurrection in the hereafter." Three paragraphs earlier in the same essay he remarked: "Movement . . . is a blessing and a source of survival and evolution, while rigidity is a cause of stasis, decline, and death."[12] Hilary Austen, author of *Artistry Unleashed: A Guide to Pursuing Great Performance in Work and Life*, pointed out—in a similar vein but in a totally different context (how unleashing the artist in a business setting

---

10. The title of the English translation—*The Seven Veils of Seth*—is based on the author's inscription in the copy of the Arabic novel he sent the translator.

11. David S. Noss, *A History of the World's Religions*, 10th ed. (Upper Saddle River, NJ: Prentice Hall, 1999), 355.

12. Mehdi Bazargan, "Religion and Liberty," in *Liberal Islam: A Sourcebook*, ed. Charles Kurzman (Oxford: Oxford University Press, 1998), 82.

can help a firm "move on")—that the opposite of chaos is not order but stagnation.[13]

WANTAHET

Al-Koni's Oasis (or New Waw) trilogy begins with *New Waw* (*Waw al-Sughra*),[14] continues with *The Puppet* (*al-Dumya*), and ends with *al-Fazza'a* (*The Scarecrow*). This eponymous protagonist of the third novel appeared in *The Puppet* to offer good advice to that novel's well-intentioned hero. In *al-Fazza'a*, though, his destruction of the oasis—which he justifies as an appropriate reward for the community's contempt for his benefactions—seems malicious and vengeful.[15] A voice in the crowd at a food distribution in this novel warns that this may be another version of Wantahet's infamous banquet, and the chapter called "Wantahet" gives a version of this famous banquet as part of a folktale about a contest between proponents respectively of anger, envy, hatred, and revenge. Paradoxically, the chief vassal of New Waw remarks to its demonic ruler that by repaying good with evil he has demonstrated that he is a human being, not a demon. In al-Koni's novel *Lawn al-La'na* (*The Color of the Curse*), the demonic protagonist, who even has an evil apprentice, is so evil that the ambiguous interplay of good and evil (or between stagnation and chaos) seems lost. He is said to have sold his soul to the "Master of Dark Tyrannies" and therefore to have returned as a devil.[16] This demon in *Lawn al-La'na* is also referred to as Wantahet.[17]

Are all these demons different forms of Wantahet, who is trying to show us the way back to Waw, the real Tuareg paradise? If God is so good that He can bring good out of evil (as Thomas Aquinas argued in a passage al-Koni has used for an epigraph), should we thank God for demons? Incidentally, the demon—in at least some of al-Koni's many

---

13. Hilary Austen, interview by Peter Day on *Global Business*, BBC World Service, in an episode entitled "Thinking about Thinking," updated March 31, 2011.
14. The novel *al-Waram* (*The Tumor*), in which the ruler finds that his official robe has fused with his skin, is related to this trilogy but seems to stand outside the plot sequence of the trilogy per se. The four volumes have been marketed separately in Arabic.
15. In a private conversation at Georgetown University on April 28, 2011, Ibrahim al-Koni said he had the first international blockade of Libya in mind when he wrote *The Scarecrow*.
16. *Lawn al-La'na* (Beirut: al-Mu'assasa al-'Arabiya li-l-Dirasat wa-l-Nashr, 2005), 14.
17. Ibid., 236.

novels—is a counterweight to the tribe's leaders, not to God, and the lost Law of the Tuareg people plays the part that might elsewhere be assumed by God. In al-Koni's novel *Anubis*, moreover, the ancient goddess Tanit has top billing, not a male god or demon.

Ibrahim al-Koni obviously draws on many traditions and authors from Tuareg to Russian to Chinese and American, and adds literary and mythological allusions the way an artist applies washes or glazes to give added depth to a painting. Are al-Koni's references to Seth and other demonic figures merely mythological washes or part of a consistent storyline that forms part of his own or of Tuareg mythology?

In *The Seven Veils of Seth*, the chief of the oasis community teases his visitor: "How can you expect our elders not to think ill of you when you arrive on the back of a jenny, as if you were the accursed Wantahet, who has been the butt of jokes for generations?"[18] As their exchange continues, the chief reminds the visitor: "The strategist known as Wantahet also claimed he would carry people on the path of deliverance the day he cast them down the mouth of the abyss."[19] There is a more complete version of this accusation later in the novel: "The master of the jenny at the end of time would approach villages to entice tribes to a banquet only to pull the banquet carpet out from under them, allowing them to fall into a bottomless abyss."[20] These references to the Wantahet of Tuareg mythology appear in several of al-Koni's novels. When the translator asked Ibrahim al-Koni for further details from Tuareg folklore about Wantahet, the author replied that he starts with the folkloric scraps he has and uses them as a starting point. In his "Témoinage," al-Koni said that he has created his own desert and filled it with his own symbols and archetypes.[21]

ANCIENT EGYPT: SETH

Ancient Egyptian attitudes toward Seth underwent an evolution and are not consistent across the literature and over the centuries. Put another way: the study of Seth in ancient Egyptian religion is the domain of specialists. H. Te Velde, one such expert, in *Seth, God of Confusion* says, for example, that if "In mythology and for many Egyptians Seth" was "the

---

18. *The Seven Veils of Seth*, 75.
19. Ibid., 76.
20. Ibid., 143.
21. Al-Koni, "Témoinage," 97.

divine foreigner" or the "god of confusion, for the faithful he was also unrestrictedly god." He adds, however, that: "after the 20th dynasty" not only were "no new temples . . . built" for Seth but there is no "evidence that existing temples of Seth were restored."[22]

Isan in *The Seven Veils of Seth* is called the Jenny Master, because he rides a she-ass, and a vivid account is offered of how he learned to hate camels and love a wild she-ass.[23] Similarly, the hero of *Lawn al-La'na* is said to have traveled south to Africa's forestlands on a camel with a caravan but to have returned on a she-ass.[24] H. Te Velde in *Seth, God of Confusion* includes a chapter about the "Seth-animal," which has been connected with various mammals, real and imaginary, including the wild ass.[25] E. A. Wallis Budge in *The Gods of the Egyptians* says that "The Ass, like many animals, was regarded by Egyptians both as a god and a devil."[26] To be sure, there is also in the Islamic history of the Maghreb a famous Sahib al-Himar: Abu Yazid Mukallad ibn Kayrad al-Nukkari (d. 947 CE), a Berber who led a rebellion against Fatimid rule in what is today Tunisia. He was known as the Ass Master because he rode a donkey.

Te Velde quotes a text in which Seth announces, "I am Seth who causes confusion and thunders in the horizon of the sky. . . ."[27] Seth, then, is the lord of rain, although "in Egypt vegetation and the fertility of the soil is not dependent on rain, but on the inundation of the Nile."[28]

A potion that al-Koni's Isan slips into the pool causes women in the oasis to miscarry, but he can also cure their fertility problems. Te Velde says of Seth that he is "the god who brings about abortion."[29] Seth's method of cure underscores his sexual prowess. Te Velde says, "Seth is a god of sexuality which is not canalized into fertility."[30]

In *The Seven Veils of Seth*, both the character Isan—who doubles as Seth and Wantahet—and the repeated references to the lost Tuareg Law promote nomadism (and tribalism) and discourage settled life in an oasis

---

22. H. Te Velde, *Seth, God of Confusion* (Leiden: E. J. Brill, 1967), 138–139.
23. *The Seven Veils of Seth*, 129 ff.
24. *Lawn al-La'na*, 15.
25. Te Velde, 13–26.
26. E. A. Wallis Budge, *The Gods of the Egyptians* (1904; New York: Dover Publications, 1969), 2:367.
27. Te Velde, 106.
28. Ibid., 54.
29. Ibid., 29.
30. Ibid., 55.

where tribalism is diluted. If religions tend to promote group solidarity—whether locally or globally—it seems reasonable that a demon like Seth should, in the later eras of ancient Egypt, be portrayed as a deviant foreigner.

Te Velde explains, "Because Seth repeatedly proved to have been collaborating in maintaining the cosmic order, though in a peculiar way, Seth could be worshipped."[31] Once the worship of Seth fell from favor, however, Seth became "exclusively a demonic murderer and chaotic power. . . ."[32] and "a dreadful demon of the black magicians"[33] and thus no longer "the ancient Egyptian god of the desert and divine foreigner. . . ."[34]

If E. O. Wilson and others are correct in ascribing to religion the role of reinforcing an innate human tendency toward tribalism by encouraging human groups that prefer the group's members to outsiders,[35] then a religion's demons should also serve this purpose. Even though he is a neo-Darwinian, Wilson embraces Jung's archetypes and lists two "of the most frequently cited" as "*The Trickster*" who "disturbs established order" and "*A monster*" that "*threatens humanity* . . . (Satan writhing at the bottom of hell). . . ."[36]

Jung claimed in "Archetypes of the Collective Unconscious" that these archetypes are "primordial types . . . universal images that have existed since the remotest times."[37] If he is correct, the net must be cast over all of human experience, not simply Africa or Europe. In "On the Psychology of the Trickster-Figure" he pointed out that Yahweh in the Hebrew Bible exhibits

> not a few reminders of the unpredictable behavior of the
> trickster, of his senseless orgies of destruction . . . together
> with the same gradual development into a savior and his
> simultaneous humanization. It is just this transformation
> of the meaningless into the meaningful that reveals the
> trickster's compensatory relation to the "saint."[38]

---

31. Ibid., 140.
32. Ibid., 141.
33. Ibid., 148.
34. Ibid., 147.
35. Edward O. Wilson, *Consilience: The Unity of Knowledge* (1998; New York: Vintage Books, 1999), 280–281.
36. Ibid., 244.
37. C. G. Jung, *The Archetypes and the Collective Unconscious*, vol. 9, 2nd ed., trans. R. F. C. Hull (Princeton: Princeton University Press, 1968), part 1, 4–5.
38. Ibid., 256.

One main theme of *The Scarecrow* is the humanization of the demonic protagonist. Does this transformation also help the meaningless become meaningful? If Jung was even partially correct about archetypes, then many other players can be introduced with questions like: Is Shiva's role of constructive destruction in the Hindu Trimurti similar to that played by al-Koni's demon?

WEST AFRICA

Robert D. Pelton, in his book *The Trickster in West Africa*, says that "the trickster pulls the most unyielding matter—disease, ugliness, greed, lust, lying, jealousy—into the orbit of life. . . ."[39] He also says, earlier, that "His presence . . . represents a ceaseless informing of structure with rawness and formlessness and a boundless confidence that such a process is truly constructive."[40] Roger D. Abrahams, in *African Folktales*, says of the trickster that he "represents primal creativity and pathological destructiveness, childish innocence, and self-absorption." He "lives in the wilds, but makes regular incursions into the human community . . ." and "is sexually voracious."[41] Abrahams summarizes:

> the vitality and the protean abilities of Trickster . . .
> are continually fascinating and . . . carry . . . the
> characteristic African message that life is celebrated
> most fully through the dramatizing of oppositions.[42]

Viewed from a West African perspective, the scarecrow phenomenon in the final two novels of al-Koni's Oasis trilogy (*The Puppet* and *The Scarecrow*) are masquerades, perhaps comparable to the Yoruba *egungun*, a returning ancestor. Moreover, the idea that a spirit or god may take possession of a worshiper or borrow random body parts to visit the market has a wealth of West African parallels.

---

39. Robert D. Pelton, *The Trickster in West Africa* (Berkeley: University of California Press, 1980), 252.
40. Ibid.
41. Roger D. Abrahams, *African Folktales* (New York: Pantheon Books, 1983), 155.
42. Ibid., 156.

ESHU

Eshu stands out among the 401 Yoruba orisha who either represent dimensions of Olorun, the sky god, or serve him, because Eshu acts as their messenger. Few of Africa's traditional gods are portrayed in African art, but Eshu's face is usually carved on the Ifa divination tray. God of the road, he may be worshiped at a crossroads. In the chapter called "The Scarecrow," we learn that cunning strategists in Tuareg culture are cautious at crossroads. Eshu is also a trickster who deliberately starts fights, but these fights normally promote sacrifices to the orisha—he receives a commission—and therefore improve human conduct.

Noel Q. King, in *African Cosmos*, first warns Muslims and Christians against confusing Eshu with Satan and then cautions anthropologists against seeing him as the trickster. (King refers to him instead as the Prankster—a subtle distinction.) If Eshu deceives "people into wrong behavior," that is primarily "so they may gain favor by their expiation and feed the divinities with their offerings."[43] Similarly, in his book *The Trickster in West Africa*, Robert D. Pelton says that by starting a quarrel between two friends, Eshu demonstrates that their "friendship was held together by custom, not by mutual awareness" or by "a willingness to undergo modification together."[44] Fixing a chair that was poorly repaired or a bone that was improperly set may require breaking it again first. In his excellent article about al-Koni, Sabry Hafez was, then, perhaps overly influenced by Semitic precedents when he identified the Tuareg Wantahet (*wantahit*) as "Beelzebub, the prince of the evil spirits."[45] This is odd, because on the previous page he said, "the desert's spiritual balance is maintained by an amalgam of African and ancient Egyptian tenets."[46] His reference then was, admittedly, to the role of ancestors' spirits, not to demons. A few pages later he identified Wantahet himself, specifically, as "the prince of evil spirits. . ."[47] and then after that said that one of the characters is "the personification of *wantahit*, Beelzebub."[48] A more African Wantahet

---

43. Noel Q. King, *African Cosmos: An Introduction to Religion in Africa* (Belmont, CA: Wadsworth Publishing Co., 1986), 10–11.

44. Pelton, 142.

45. Sabry Hafez, "The Novel of the Desert: Poetics of Space and Dialectics of Freedom," in *La Poétique de l'espace*, 67.

46. Ibid., 66.

47. Ibid., 76.

48. Ibid., 80

is, arguably, a more interesting (and more authentically Tuareg) literary demon. In the chapter called "Wantahet" in *The Scarecrow*, Wantahet is presented as the advocate of revenge or retribution. Thus, he plays a role parallel to that of Eshu as a trickster who rebalances the scales of justice in the novel by pulling a carpet out from under the feet of malefactors.

Pelton also says that Eshu's "presence in the market is indeed a phallic presence, loaded with volatile, unstable energy." He observes,

> Eshu embodies sexuality as unleashed desire—not lust merely, nor even avarice, envy or greed, but that passion for what lies outside one's grasp which the Greeks saw in some sense as the sovereign mover of human life.[49]

Pelton summarizes: "Eshu does not only present riddles; he is one."[50] Seth, in *The Seven Veils of Seth*, poses riddles as well and definitely is one.

Manning Marable in *Malcolm X: A Life of Reinvention* at one point calls Malcolm X a North American version of a West African trickster, saying that Malcolm X:

> presented himself as the embodiment of the two central figures of African-American folk culture, simultaneously the hustler/trickster and the preacher/minister. Janus-faced, the trickster is unpredictable, capable of outrageous transgressions; the minister saves souls, redeems shattered lives, and promises a new world.[51]

These roles are precisely—albeit perhaps coincidentally—the two sides of Isan's character in *The Seven Veils of Seth*, of the mythic Wantahet character in Tuareg folklore, and of al-Koni's demons, as in *The Scarecrow*.

One other parallel to African American culture is the occasional use by al-Koni of call-and-response passages like the second section of the second chapter, "The Prophecy," in *The Scarecrow*.

49. Ibid., 161.
50. Ibid., 162.
51. Manning Marable, *Malcolm X: A Life of Reinvention* (New York: Viking, 2011), 11.

AL-KONI'S MYSTICAL, SUFI, AND EUROPEAN FORMATION

Seth and Eshu, admittedly, may not have been the only inspirations for the development of the demonic hero in the novels of al-Koni, because other forces—like Sufism and Russian literature—have also been part of his formation.

Ziad Elmarsafy, in his book *Sufism in the Contemporary Arabic Novel*, has an elegant chapter devoted to demonstrating the central place of Sufism not only in the novels of Ibrahim al-Koni but in explaining his sense of mission as a novelist. He refers, for example, to al-Koni's motif of "the wanderings of individuals in the desert" as "a mystical ecology."[52] He says that "Al-Koni's use of Sufi elements is present in his writings from the outset."[53] Moreover, "It is no accident that his repertoire of stock characters includes . . . the spiritual master and the disciple."[54] Although Wantahet in al-Koni's novels is accused of inviting people to a banquet on a carpet spread over an abyss, Elmarsafy explains: "Al-Koni makes clear that the abyss (*al-hawiya*) is a key step in a spiritual journey, during which the traveller's suffering is at its worst."[55] This Sufi interpretation of the abyss totally transforms the meaning of Wantahet's banquet. Referring to the division of the Tuareg world into a visible and an invisible sphere, Elmarsafy summarizes a discussion of the subject by Hélène Claudot-Hawad and repeats her point that it is the Sufi, not the tribal leader, who can move between the two spheres.[56] Wantahet then becomes a Sufi prototype, and *al-hawiya*—the abyss or pit beneath the banquet blanket—becomes one of the stages on the Sufi path. Thus Wantahet's invitation to the abyss becomes an invitation to a form of union with the divine. A member of the Council of Elders says in *The Scarecrow*: "We must accept the abyss if the fall into it has been willed by the Spirit World."

Iblis, who in Islamic belief is the chief devil, has a better reputation with some Sufis than with Shari'ah-minded, act-right Muslims, precisely because he refused to bow to anyone save God. Thus, arguably, he was the sincerest monotheist. Moreover, the Beloved's curse bestows enviable

---

52. Ziad Elmarsafy, *Sufism in the Contemporary Arabic Novel* (Edinburgh: Edinburgh University Press, 2012), 107.
53. Ibid., 108.
54. Ibid., 110.
55. Ibid., 129.
56. Ibid., 112.

recognition on the lover, because it shows God's interest in that individual. In Farid ud-Din Attar's *The Conference of the Birds*, for example, Eblis (Iblis) says: "All creatures seek throughout the universe/What will be mine for ever now—Your curse!"[57] Finally, Elmarsafy has several pages of analysis of what he terms al-Koni's own "Sufi Autobiography," *Marathi Ulis*.[58]

Attar's ambivalence about Satan, the ultimate monotheist, is only part of the problem, as Afkham Darbandi and Dick Davis point out in their introduction when they refer to "the Sufi love of paradox" being deployed as "a way of jolting the reader out of his normal expectations of the world. . . ." Furthermore, they warn that "Objects and individuals don't maintain their allegorical significance from one story to another, so the meanings of the symbols in each story have to be worked out anew."[59]

Another element of al-Koni's formation has been Russian literature, including authors like Dostoyevsky. Al-Koni has written of his "specific and intimate" relationship with Dostoyevsky, whom he has referred to as his master. He highlights the influence on him of Dostoyevsky's "philosophic dimension and his symbolic system." In this context, al-Koni says that a novel can be considered "ideas transformed into life" and that no other novelist was able to treat "abstract ideas and incarnate them in life" better than Dostoyevsky.[60]

Marc Slonim, in his introduction to an English translation of *The Brothers Karamazov*, brings attention to human transgression:

> The compulsion toward transgression . . . was to Dostoyevsky, a basic human compulsion; man does not accept his condition, nor does he accept the world which determined this condition.[61]

In *The Scarecrow*'s chapter called "The Gifts," the newly anointed demonic ruler tempts the elders, who have proclaimed him leader of Waw,

---

57. Farid ud-Din Attar, *The Conference of the Birds*, trans. Afkham Darbandi & Dick Davis, rev. ed. (London: Penguin Books, 2011), 182. See also Faridu'd-Din Attar, *The Speech of the Birds*, trans. P. W. Avery (Cambridge, UK: The Islamic Texts Society, 1998), 293 for a less memorable but more complete translation of the same passage.

58. Elmarsafy, 130–138.

59. Attar, xvii–xviii.

60. Al-Koni, "Témoinage," 101.

61. Marc Slonim, introduction to *The Brothers Karamazov*, by Fyodor Dostoyevsky (New York: The Modern Library, 1950), ix.

with gifts from his wonder-sack, exactly as if he were Mephistopheles tempting Faust.

CONCLUSION

All these extra varnishes or glazes on the painted surface of some of Ibrahim al-Koni's novels enhance and reinforce the image of al-Koni's demon as an agent of chaos construed as creative disorder, which is destabilizing but also necessary for growth—economic, physical, or spiritual. In *The Scarecrow*, once the demon becomes a despot, some of the balance or tension may be lost. The term theosis in Eastern Christianity refers to the doctrine asserting that if God can become man, men can become godlike. In al-Koni's novels, if man can become demonic, jinnis can become human. There is no abyss or Sufi salvation under a carpet at the end of *The Scarecrow*, and the senior demon in *Lawn al-La'na* may be the least interesting of al-Koni's demons because he is so monochromatic, so evil.

Ancient Egyptian and West African sacred stories (myths) can serve as points of reference for interpreting demonic humans and humane demons in the works of Ibrahim al-Koni. Recent history, though, is also relevant. In a series of telephone conversations, Ibrahim al-Koni told the translator frequently that he is not a political person and not a political author. All the same, Colonel Qaddafi was, he has also said, one of *The Scarecrow*'s multiple inspirations. Since the Arabic novel was completed and published in 1998, the crisis at the end refers not to the Libyan leader's final year but to an earlier confrontation between Libya and the international community. The scarecrow (or Wantahet) and Qaddafi may have shared some West African characteristics: eccentricity that verges on the criminal, virility or male sexuality separated from fertility, self-centered exploitation of a culture of individual empowerment, encouragement or exploitation of tribalism, the embrace of nomadism or at least of the tent as a personal symbol, and acceptance of the role of Nietzsche's *Übermensch* (or overman), whose antics, however deadly, never truly threaten the survival of the herd—or at least did not threaten it until the invention of weapons of mass destruction.

In short, a much fuller, more nuanced portrait of Wantahet and his avatars—who are frequent visitors to Ibrahim al-Koni's novels—is provided by looking outside the traditional characterization of Satan by the three main Abrahamic religions.

In *The Fetishists*, al-Koni had Adda, the leader, explain: "Goodness, like truth, is an angel that speeds unimpeded across the countryside, but when a human hand seizes it and places it in a flask, it turns into an evil demon."[62]

---

62. Ibrahim al-Koni, *al-Majus*, 4th printing (Beirut: al-Multaka Publishing, 2001), 47.

THE SCARECROW

We are the hollow men
We are the stuffed men
Leaning together
Headpiece filled with straw. Alas!

T. S. Eliot, "The Hollow Men"

Some weave huge figures of wicker,
and fill their limbs with live humans,
who are then burned to death when the figures are set afire.

Julius Caesar, *The Gallic War* Book VI.16

With an ill omen you take home a woman
whom Greece will come to claim with a great army. . . .

Horace, *Odes I: Carpe Diem* Song 15

THE OMEN

1

"Taking the matter seriously is actually a grave threat."

The hero repeated this phrase twice and pulled from his pocket a scrap of blue cloth that he wound carefully around his right index finger. Then he began to wipe his eyelids very cautiously.

Across the room from him, the chief merchant said, "The threat does not lie in taking it seriously. The danger comes from another site that is closer to us than our jugular veins."

The council members gazed at him with interest, but he did not turn to face his peers. Instead he traced a symbol on the ground with his finger and then concluded cryptically, "The threat lies in the title!"

More than one voice asked, "The title?"

"In the awe-inspiring title of leader."

They exchanged covert glances, and the hero interjected, "You're right! The tribes have learned from long experience that a man remains a man like any other until the Spirit World tests him with leadership. Afterward he is changed and transformed much as nursing infants are when their mothers neglect them and leave them in areas that aren't safeguarded by knife blades. I think our late comrade is a prime example of what I'm talking about."

They retreated into silence again. They traveled far away, wandering in other realms. They circled the deserts and descended into the caverns. The cavern into which suspicious people descend during hours of despondency, however, is not merely enveloped in gloom—it is also bottomless, because it is a cavern that is not temporally perceived or located in space.

Even so, the peers heard a voice issue from Imaswan Wandarran's cavern: "What is the secret reason for the change, I wonder? Shouldn't we consider this a symptom of a major defect?"

From the cavern symbolized by the cryptic mark he had traced in the dirt with his finger, the man with two veils spoke again. "We wrong the man on whom we bestow the title of leader if we think he possesses a choice in the matter. We forget that the leader is a miserable creature because he isn't his own master."

He fell silent. Ah'llum urged him to clarify his statement: "Take one more step, because we haven't understood."

"'*Areyakhrakan yaqled Anhi*. He who has lost his way should consult Anhi.' This is what the Lost Book teaches us in its laws. We forget that leadership is a form of sovereignty, and that sovereignty is as haunted a place as the site of a treasure."

Imaswan Wandarran cried out, "Did you call sovereignty a haunted site?"

"If the Spirit World's tribes seized control of gold in the first age, and forbade its use by anyone else in the ancient covenant our forefathers discussed in our lost Law, the jinn had already seized control of leadership long before that. They singled out sovereignty as their homeland before they ever seized control of gold dust."

"Reports of an irrevocable gold-dust covenant between our forefathers and the people of the Spirit Word have reached us, but we have never previously heard of a group seizing control of sovereignty."

More than one voice moaned appreciatively in support of their comrade's clarification. So the chief merchant continued his struggle to reveal the secret of leadership with the keys provided by talismans he had drawn in the dirt.

"It is right for a merchant to discuss haunted homelands, because merchants are the only community that uses a haunted currency for their transactions. Yes, yes: treasures are our currency, and leadership is not merely the mainstay of treasure, which is what the masses imagine, but actually the secret of the treasure, the mate of the treasure, and the head of the treasure."

He buried legions of talismans beneath a pile of dirt and plucked from the earth a handful of pebbles of different colors. He heaped these in his palm and gazed at them absentmindedly.

From an unidentified cavern a voice called out, "In the time when rocks were moist and the earth was inhabited only by the people of the Spirit World, Grandfather Mandam descended to it after he was exiled from his unidentified homeland. Dressed in the rags of desert nomads, the jinn went out to meet him. They had decided to offer a little secret to this migrant, who was exhausted by the curse of interminable travel.

They told their guest that they were the desert's masters and that if he wished to enjoy living in their kingdom, he merely had to obey their Law and accept a covenant whereby the son of the desert lands would become lord of these lands but leave the affairs of the spiritual worlds to the inhabitants of those worlds. Then curiosity gnawed on the human being's heart. So he asked these people what the spiritual worlds hid. Their leader's cryptic reply has been passed down through the generations. It is said that the jinn's leader declared to our ancient ancestor on that day, 'Our distinguished guest errs if he asks this, but we should excuse him, since we understand that his curiosity was the sole reason for his banishment. So know, then, that should you learn this, your knowledge would not increase but decrease and what you learn would harm you. The spiritual worlds we inhabit are the abode of the wilderness that the desert and the desert people, who will descend from your loins, occupy. The spiritual worlds are not merely a home for the empty land; they stand supreme over its head. So you must entrust your affairs to the spiritual worlds forever and never raise your head—if you want to enjoy your stay in your new homeland. If you are arrogant and wish to impose yourself as sovereign over the sovereignty of the spiritual worlds, evil will track you down, and you will suffer. So beware!' The immigrant, who was footloose by nature, did not merely dare to raise his head and walk proudly in the desert, thinking he would reach as high as the mountains, but began to strive to devise a path for himself to the heavens. He whispered, hinted, and searched for a secret that could convey him to the spiritual worlds so he could seize control of them, because he realized that human beings would never be able to possess the wilderness if they didn't find a way to seize control of the spiritual worlds. The people of the Spirit World thought they would punish this upstart for his violation of the covenant. So they allowed him to fall asleep. Then they excised his heart, which they replaced with a different one. They removed his brain and substituted another one. They amputated his hand and grafted another in its place. When the upstart woke, he found that the compassion in his heart had fled and been replaced by cruelty, that wisdom had quit his head and left in its stead stupidity and delusion, and that his right hand—which had been loath to reach up to chase a fly from his face—now rushed to slay everything in the desert. His tongue declared blasphemously that day: 'I am sovereign over the earth. I am lord of all creatures. Haven't the people of the Spirit World left me in the desert as their lieutenant? Didn't the lords of the spiritual worlds install me as lord over the wilderness?' On that ill-omened day, the upstart did not merely lift his head to boast before the heavens but also used his hand to slay. He killed—for the first time in the history of the desert. Since that day, killing has become one of the laws that rulers follow. Since that day, replacing leaders has become a favorite pastime for inhabitants of the Spirit World."

The chief merchant leaned over the pebbles, which had colors that people of the desert usually found only in beads, and covered this pile with the palm of his other hand. He began to crush the pebbles together between his two hands as if this were a ritual associated with some magic spell.

The members of the council fell prey to despondency, but Amasis the Younger waddled toward the chief merchant, dropped to his knees, and stuck out his neck to scrutinize his neighbor with a very long, inquisitive look, which not only suggested curiosity but also the suspicion that leaps from the eyes of people when they converse with individuals of dubious mental acuity. Finally Amasis, as if whispering a blandishment into the ear of a girlfriend, asked, "What are you trying to say?"

Stillness overwhelmed the council, and the members' fingers ceased furrowing the dirt, fiddling with pieces of stone, or fingering the hems of their garments. This time the men held their breath—not to quench the thirst of base curiosity, which can never be quenched, but from a desire for the wisdom hidden in the folds of a proverb and from their yearning to acquire the truth to which the Law's counsel alluded.

At that hour, the cunning strategist realized that the time had come, because his slow deliberation had realized its goal and hearts had emptied of the markets' babble and of worldly whispers. Purity had washed their hearts and prepared people to learn. So he spoke.

As he clenched his fist around his amulet and gazed at the elders even more mysteriously, he said, "Beware of binding the cord of insanity round the neck of anyone you love!"

As if waving his protest in the face of the man seated there, Imaswan Wandarran sprang into the debate: "What does this mean? What are you trying to say?"

"If you allow one among you to go there, you should realize that you will lose him forever—just as you lost poor Aggulli."

"Aggulli was stubborn, arrogant, and duplicitous."

"Everyone who goes to sit on that ill-omened throne will be stubborn, arrogant, and duplicitous."

"What's the secret reason for that, I wonder? Is it reasonable for one of us to lose his reason when he gains that title, even though he knows the whole affair from start to finish is nothing but a game within a game?"

"We will find an excuse for the wretch when we learn that he acts involuntarily."

"Did you say 'involuntarily'?"

"Our life in the desert lands is a game, but life in the spiritual lands is never a game. The man who goes to sit on the sovereign's throne is possessed by inhabitants of the Spirit World. He must see things with the eye of the Spirit World, not with the eye of the wasteland's people. This is where the calamity starts, because the wretch must believe a matter that we see by the Law of this worldly life to be a lie. So from the day the haunted piece of cloth becomes part of him, he becomes a puppet in the hand of the Spirit World, which does not see that life is a game, that the sovereign is a puppet, or that there is no place in its Law for anything besides a seriousness that surpasses by many times the seriousness we boast of. Our error comes from treating the sovereign as if he were the person we knew yesterday. We do not realize that he isn't merely another man—who bears no relationship to the man we used to know—but that he retains no relationship to any part of our world. From today forward we must be aware that the man we choose to command us is not simply lost to us forever but becomes another creature who never knew us and whom we haven't previously known. For this reason, we shouldn't expect compassion or any good from him. Indeed, we ought to expect evil. So will you insist on turning one of our peers, whose presence with us in this council delights us, into our worst enemy?"

Imaswan Wandarran turned toward his fellows and glanced absentmindedly at their faces in turn as if waiting for one of them to bring him an argument quickly or to take his side in the debate.

Finally he moved to confront his adversary with a painful question: "If what you say is true, then we treated our late comrade very unjustly."

The man with two veils responded with a courage that the tribes were unaccustomed to hearing from the tongues of merchants: "Do you doubt that?"

"Are we murderers?"

"Do you doubt that?"

Imaswan looked at his mates' faces in succession as if appealing for help, but their countenances were stern, mute, glum, expressionless masks, as if the jinn had replaced his friends and inserted creatures of their ilk into the council. He turned to confront the seated man again and stared at his face for a long time, as if seeing him for the first time.

In a peculiar tone he asked, "Do you remember the day when you surrounded us with proletarian armies who demanded that we leave the affairs of the dead to the dead and appoint the living to oversee the living?"

The chief merchant nodded his head yes but did not stop playing with the handful of pebbles in the palm of his left hand. So Imaswan resumed his questioning in the same tone: "I asked you then where you had come from, but you did not reply. Can you answer me today?"

The seated man looked up from his game inquisitively. Then Imaswan leaned toward him as if intending to butt him with his turbaned head. Staring at him provocatively, he asked, "Who are you? Who are you?"

The man with two veils shot him a proud, disparaging glance. Then he turned his attention back to the bits of rock. But Imaswan did not yield. With childish insistence he asked again, "Tell me: are you really one of the people of the wasteland or are you one of the people of the Spirit World?"

2

"If what you say about the sovereign is correct, how was our leader who sleeps in the neighboring tomb able to assume leadership one day with a finesse that hostile tribes acknowledged even before the tongues of the generations forwarded that praise—without being afflicted with the Spirit World's lunacy, which you discussed?"

The council members backed Ah'llum with a murmur of approval while the hero thrust his hand into his pocket to pull out the dark scrap of cloth that he used to daub his eyes during anxious moments—on the advice of the herbalist, who had claimed that the fabric, which was saturated with blue dye, had a magical effect and could relieve pain temporarily from his eyes and over time would heal their underlying ailment.

The council had convened many times in the temple, and the members' voices had been raised in dispute there. The sessions had been dissolved just as frequently, without the members reaching a consensus on a new governor. Neither the logic of the chief merchant nor the adage of this inscrutable man (whom they had found among them one day without knowing where he had come from or to which clan he belonged) disturbed them so much as their comrade Aggulli's fate, which seemed to presage their own, should a thirst for sovereignty get the better of them and they aspire to become the ruler.

On this day, when they reconvened, they discovered for the first time that whispers and doubts had demoralized them. They listened apprehensively to each other and were wary about what was said, as one comrade looked at another with a cautious eye.

Before the man with two veils rushed to respond, the hero asked him for a slight clarification: "You should realize that I'm not discussing the characteristics of the leader of yesteryear to rehash the generation's legends or to confirm the views of the masses, who did not know him. I said what I said, because the Spirit World rewarded me by making me a member of this noble council when I was young."

The chief merchant glared at him malevolently. He toyed with the edge of his lower veil to mask his reaction before he responded to the question with a question: "Did you find in the late leader the traits of leadership during all the time you associated with him?"

"What do you mean to say?"

"Was the leader in the tomb a leader like all the others?"

"What do you want to say?"

"I am saying that the leader of eternity was a poet before he became a leader. The invisible jinni called 'poetry' in our language conquered in his chest the ghoul we call 'leadership' in our miserable language."

"It is said that he recited charming poems in his youth, and I don't deny that in my youth I recited couplets the tribe attributed to him. Everyone knows, however, that the Council of Wisdom stifled the gift in him because it thought poetry a game ill befitting a leader's majesty. Similarly, on another day, it stifled in his chest his desire to marry the poet, because it thought that she too was a caprice inappropriate for the grandeur of the leader."

"The sages stifled in his chest the poetry of the tongue, but his poetry flowed out in his deeds and traits."

"Why not dam the flood head on? Why do you want to tire our heads with hard puzzles? Here, I'll dam the flow and say that anyone who has settled in the Spirit World to become a poet doesn't need to change and disguise himself from the world—unlike a worldly leader. The secret doesn't lie in his being someone who lives only for play—as befits any ruler—but in his being someone who has known from the beginning that he will govern a wasteland in which he discovers the clearly visible face of the Spirit World."

"Everyone who knew him will acknowledge that he never was playful."

"Did you all spy on his heart too, the way you spied on him whenever he stood up or sat down, went or came?"

"Playfulness, like passionate love, cannot be concealed."

"The wise way he ruled the tribe proves that he wasn't merely playful but a cunning strategist too."

"People who knew him never found him to be anything but a shining exemplar of earnestness and an icon of severity."

"Severity flourishes only in the meadows of playfulness."

"Here we return to riddles via the widest portal!"

"The playfulness to which we refer isn't the sport of young minds, which is what the masses assume. It is, instead, a great secret no less significant than the Law itself."

". . . ."

"If the question of playfulness were insignificant, people wouldn't have cursed life and wouldn't have found happiness to be harder to achieve than passing a camel's neck through the eye of a needle."

"Do you consider play really to be this difficult?"

"Play, like prophecy, is a heavenly firebrand. If it could be grasped by anyone hustling and bustling on earth, happiness would have been easy."

"Amazing!"

"Our master, who slumbers nearby, didn't go to the distant sanctuary to snatch the gift using the sovereignty of the intellect; he did that following the path of a possessed person who went to reclaim a bequest left to him by his ancestors."

"His ancestors?"

"The Spirit World. For a man obsessed by poetry, the Spirit World is, quite simply, his homeland. I mean that a poet obtains by inspiration what sages do not obtain through the sovereignty of the intellect."

"Do you think so highly of poets?"

"The poet is the only man about whom there is no fear of his becoming lost in the labyrinth, because he is the only creature who came to this wasteland as a lost wanderer."

"We merely need to search for a poet to rule over us on our behalf."

"I fear you won't be able to find the poet I am talking about."

"You shouldn't think so poorly of us."

"I also fear that our comrade may have gotten ahead of me and thought ill of our master who reclines in the tomb, if he thinks that the leader of eternity deserves the title of poet merely because he amused himself with some vile verses in his youth."

"The fact is that I have almost lost my way again. . . ."

"I was trying to say that our leader was a true poet. I mean he wasn't a poet because he recited couplets about passionate love or some other inane subject; he was a poet greater than all the others whom desert tribes have known, because he dandled in his heart a treasure named 'nobility.'"

"It won't be difficult for us to find among the people a poet who hides in his heart this quality that you call a treasure."

"Far from it!"

"What do you mean?"

"I fear we will never be able to."

"Is it reasonable for us to lack a single noble person in all these dwellings?"

"What I really fear is talking constantly with two different tongues."

Their comrade fell silent, and stillness pervaded the meeting.

Outside, in a place near the temple's walls, a muffled, evil, hoarse chortle echoed, immediately reminding listeners of the ignoble laughter that passersby commonly heard when they approached the mysterious scarecrow placed in the fields.

3

"If leadership is so hazardous and dangerous, then our only choice is to go with the slumbering leader."

Amasis the Younger, out of all the council members, was the man most inclined to yield and most cautious about speaking his mind. So his peers were astonished on each of the infrequent occasions when he allowed himself to leave the redoubt of silence to divulge a diffident opinion to them.

Astonishment washed over them on this day too, and they exchanged meaningful looks. The silence, however, did not last long because this notion provoked a reaction from the chief merchant, who snapped at his colleague's face: "I find it odd that you did not discern this idea's danger before allowing it to spill from your tongue."

"Danger?"

"The gravest danger! Did you, like many others, think me stupid the day I relied on the support of the masses to impose on the council the choice of a puppet who stumbles over the earth on two feet?"

"Actually, I still find it odd that you should have been the first to request a puppet who stumbles on two feet yesterday but today come to threaten us with how dangerous it is to sit on the throne of leadership."

"What I did yesterday was motivated by a desire to advance commerce, to advance the life of this oasis. What I am saying today about sovereignty stems from a fear that you will all suffer the same fate as Aggulli. Do you find fault with this?"

"No one is finding fault, but it isn't hard for someone listening to all of you argue to realize that the easiest alternative is for us to rely on the rock of the tomb and to seek a prophecy as we did in the past and as our ancestors did before us."

"I wasn't discussing leadership to scare you. I sincerely wished to call your attention to a secret quality that the Spirit World has placed in sovereignty, ever since people first found a sovereign over their heads."

"No one questions your intentions, but it's hard for anyone to accept the label 'murderer.'"

The man with two veils cast him a disparaging look and said sarcastically, "Although I admit you were the last to plant the blade in the victim's heart, I fear that your hesitation won't wipe the dead man's blood from your hands."

The hero interjected, "We must stop this. We didn't come to discuss something we did with a single hand to rescue the life of the oasis."

The chief merchant raised his voice argumentatively: "Why are voices raised in the council in an attempt to send us back today to a place we left yesterday, if our objective truly is advancing the life of the oasis?"

Ah'llum asked, "To what place is our colleague referring?"

"Doesn't our friend wish us to give up and revert to the old way?"

"We all believe that an oasis without a governor is like a headless body. We all know that commerce without a master is like a herd without a herdsman, because we have become entrepreneurs—like all the other residents of the oasis. But we must find a way to escape from our dilemma. Why don't you finally say which of us you think is best qualified to become the governor?"

Awaiting a reply, they directed heads wrapped in veils toward their colleague, but the chief merchant's eyes fled to the ceiling, and his right hand repeatedly massaged his left wrist. Then, with the cryptic phrasing of a diviner attempting to discern a prophecy in the void, he said, "I fear the best plan would be to confer leadership on someone who is not present with us now."

Imaswan Wandarran clapped his hands together and shouted, "Lately riddles seem destined to become our language."

Ah'llum, however, gestured for him not to be hasty. Like someone sighting the bearer of glad tidings in the distance, he told the chief merchant: "Not so fast! Slow down! I think I have found the talisman's key. I bet you're referring to the venerable elder. Am I right?"

A smile glinted in the eyes of the man with two veils, and rubbing his hands together jubilantly he returned from his journey to the ceiling. "You're right. I actually didn't mean any other creature."

The council members exchanged glances that were a confused mixture of anxiety and astonishment. Ah'llum entered the fray with a solemn question: "Are you mocking us?"

Fiddling with his hands, the chief merchant replied frigidly, "Mocking you never once crossed my mind."

"But . . . but I'm sure you realize that the venerable elder has had no foothold in our world for a very long time."

"A person without a foothold in our world is the most appropriate creature to head our world."

"Are you mocking us?"

"Have you forgotten that I once said in this council that our mistake lay in continuing to treat commanders in chief like creatures of our world, when everything shows that they become creatures of another type, tracing their descent to alternative homelands, the day they consent to don the mantles of leadership?"

"Emmamma has quit all homelands. Emmamma has lived on the borders of the Spirit World for a long time. How can someone who has taken the Spirit World for a homeland become our governor? How can we convince people that this is right? How can we deflect their scorn? How can we shield ourselves against their anger?"

"This is the goal. The aim is for us to allow people of eternity to enjoy their absence in eternity and to leave the affairs of this world to people of the world."

"What are you saying?"

"Only a person who has traversed a long stage in the Unknown can realize that our world is a game inside a game."

"Won't you proceed a stage further so we may understand the talisman's allusion?"

"I'm saying that the venerable elder Emmamma is the only creature who will not contest sovereignty with us—not because he isn't interested in the earth's thrones but because he exists outside the physical world."

"Ha, ha, ha . . . I admit this is a sordid plan!"

"This will shield us from the error we committed the day we made Aggulli our leader, and repeating mistakes is a foul deed that ill befits the people's sages."

"Bravo! Bravo! Now the council can cheer with me, because thanks to this judicious plan, we won't merely obviate a matter that has caused us trouble all this time, we will also be able to say that we've achieved an epiphany."

He turned to face the council, gazing happily, comprehensively, and childishly at its members. Then he shouted, "Rejoice at the good news: from today forward you, collectively, are the governor. Ha, ha. . . . Each of you from today on is a leader. We'll grant the title to the venerable elder, because that poor man won't need anything but the title. We'll retain the amulet and divide up the booty. What a plan! What a scheme! Ha, ha. . . . I admit once more that you are a grander schemer than all the others. But . . . but, why weren't we able to hit upon this division of power before?"

He continued to guffaw as the edge of his lower veil slipped down. The linen revealed an ugly mouth that looked like a female bosom. On top, it was bounded by a bushy mustache streaked with gray. Below, it was besieged by the jungles of a bushy, very gray beard. Anyone who saw this mouth understood the secret reason for the desert people's invention of this wrapped veil, which became their trademark among all the tribes.

He extended a trembling hand to hide a crack the Law had reckoned tantamount to genitalia even before people came to see it as disgraceful.

He shouted again, "Send at once for the venerable elder!"

4

The venerable elder is said to have adopted a litter for a bed long before old age vanquished him and he was no longer able to walk. So he had become the first to recline on a wooden frame supported by the necks of slaves.

Apparently this invention aroused the admiration of the noblemen and the lords of commerce in the oasis, because they adopted it from him and competed with each other to accessorize it with rows of lucky charms, other amulets designed to ward off evil, wild animal skins imported from the southern forestlands and adorned with symbols of gods, magical designs, and celestial bodies outlined with colored beads. The nobles climbed onto these wooden frames and had slaves and mamluks carry them on their shoulders as they toured the alleys, markets, fields, and plazas to flaunt what they owned. Such opulent litters put to shame the venerable elder's meager, bare sticks, which had been crisscrossed into a lattice by admirers' hands and covered with a glabrous old goatskin mat. Thus Emmamma's convoy no longer attracted the attention of passersby or sparked curiosity in the breasts of the masses, as it once had, when their eyes spotted this load transported on the heads of two dark, bare-shouldered mamluks of different heights.

Even when the sorcerers' prophecies came true and the inhabitants of the oasis saw with their own eyes the unfolding of those phases this coterie believe are a gambit concealed in the life of each person who is destined to live a long time so that he may be born a second time, and when people witnessed the transformation in the venerable elder's body (which sprouted black hair and teeth with a gleam, whiteness, and soundness that rivaled those of boys and which shed its pathetic skin that resembled a mass of palm-fiber rope or wrappings made from acacia bark, sloughing it off the way a serpent sloughs off its scales for a new skin that seems so alive it resembles the temptation leaping from belles' faces), this glorious birth, this "second birth" as sorcerers call it, could not persuade Emmamma to descend from his mobile throne and to dismount from his glorious litter, which was supported by the necks of sturdy men. His refusal to walk was not because of the custom that turned free men into slaves and not because he thought himself more entitled to the throne that he had created one day than copycats who had adopted it and then had soon started competing with each other to adorn it the way women's hands adorn the bride's face on her wedding night—even boasting that they owned it and bragging to people about its beauty the way they vaunted their possessions and children.

The slaves, instead, reported a different view from their master. They said Emmamma would not abandon the stretcher—which had become his bed, house, homeland, and bride by night and day—until this second birth also provided him with the energy of a boy who can hop through the open countryside on one foot. The set of poles represented for him—at that time when he had absented himself from time and retreated into eternity's tenebrous obscurities—the sepulcher of everlasting solitude. A man who has a natural propensity for generously making sacrificial offerings can forget everything and sacrifice everything but does not forget the person who consoled him in a time of trial and does not sacrifice the prop that has protected him from his fear of chaos in a time of forgetfulness.

The citizens did not understand the allusions of the venerable elder's language, nor did they ever comprehend the ring of pain in his immortal moan. Similarly, on that day they did not understand his cryptic prophecy, which he released to the face of the oasis after returning from the realms of the Unknown: "I wish I had never seen you. I wish I had never known you and never known your world. I wish I had never lost my world. I wish I had never returned. I wish I had never been born. I wish I had never been born. I wish I had never been born." Inquisitive minds asked him which birth he was referring to: "Today's birth or yesterday's?" His only reply was his time-honored, distressing groan, the secret meaning of which no one could ever decipher—neither in the generations living in the time of his first birth nor in the subsequent generations who were contemporaries of his second birth.

The nobles were the only ones who did not acknowledge any rebirth for the venerable elder.

The nobles described second birth as a superstition and qualified it with the adjective "purported," to disparage the masses' claims and to mock the exaggerations of people whose thirst for a prodigy was never quenched and who concocted one canard after the other.

The nobles said that the body's transformation, the skin's change, the growth of teeth or hair (or any other such phenomenon), which were characteristics they often found in desert trees and in species of camel, were no proof of a man's rebirth—as the coteries of sorcerers had claimed. Because they frequented the venerable elder more than anyone else, and as time passed learned his secret better than anyone else, they were able to assert today, too, that the venerable elder had not returned from exile in the everlasting, had not migrated from the nook of forgetfulness, had not fallen back even one step into the world of human beings, and that his phrase—which many tongues repeated and in which simpletons detected a prophecy that expressed disgust at the horror of a return after an absence—was a phrase that might be heard from the mouth of a crazed person, the throat of a feverish man transported by a trance, or the breast of a poet overcome by yearning.

The elders said that the real treasure was the intellect and that they were the men who had repeatedly conversed with Emmamma and had attempted to find in him the purported rebirth that commoners discussed but had never harvested from his tongue any trace of a rebirth of his intellect. They were justified, therefore, in ignoring the masses' claims just as they always ignored their rumors and other assertions, and had grown used to ignoring the venerable elder's distressing moans over the past years, leaving him in the corner as an ornament and protective amulet for the council—as they always said.

When citizens inquired about the secret of the venerable elder's recovery of his sense of sight (a sense that those who knew him personally asserted he had never lost), the elders responded to the question with a question: "If Emmamma has recovered his sense of sight thanks to the purported rebirth, why hasn't he regained his sense of hearing too?"

5

"Today the council is entitled to convey glad tidings to a person who has always been an amulet for the council's head," Imaswan Wandarran bellowed into the venerable elder's ear and then leaned back to sit erect. He snuck a glance at the man with two veils and then finally heard the response of the scion of eternity: "Oo . . . oo . . . oo . . . oo . . . ooh. . . ."

He groaned for a long time and swayed right and left as he customarily did when a powerful sorrow overwhelmed him. Then he proceeded to release a moan of multiple pains, repeating it with the intoxication of the possessed till it slipped out of the council, circulated through the crannies, and descended to the realms. Then the Spirit World lodged it in the expanse of the homelands. The moan finally rose into the void—heartrendingly, feverishly, piercingly, like every ancient tune.

The moan departed, but its echo lingered in the air. Then the frail body lying in a heap on the rows of poles responded to the echo with a shudder like that of people dancing ecstatically.

Imaswan looked at all his colleagues in turn and then leaned toward his neighbor's ear to elucidate the significance of the message: "Today the council can boast to the other tribes about the selection of our master to head the council. So may we hear from his mouth a thought about this puny gift?"

"Hey . . . ey . . . ey . . . ey . . . ey. . . ."

Imaswan exchanged a look with the council members and then leaned back toward the scrawny body that time had consumed till it resembled a sheaf of straw. He thrust his mouth to Emmamma's ear till his lips touched the venerable elder's veil, from which desert suns had sucked the blue color till it faded, vanished, and turned a melancholy white.

He shouted in a repulsive voice: "Do I understand from this cry that our master endorses the council's choice?"

"Ah . . . ah . . . ah . . . ah . . . ah . . . ah . . . ah . . . ah. . . ."

The cry became a genuine song—like the opening of the grief-filled ballads that the tribes' women poets call *asahagh*. Then the wasted body began to rock to the cry's beat.

Imaswan watched him with despair. Then he retreated. From the precincts of the council a voice rose: "Our master is tiring himself."

The peers looked up to find standing above them a dark giant whose black tunic's sleeves revealed muscular arms on which lingered the murky glow that gleams on the skins of intensely black lizards. In this spectral giant the noblemen recognized the mamluk who bore the venerable elder's stretcher and who always walked at the front while his shorter partner always walked at the rear. It was said that Emmamma had established this rule ages ago to keep his head raised high and thus allow him to watch the ebb and flow of creatures with his sharp, beady eyes, which the ghoul of time had vanquished—along with every other part of him.

In response to people's questioning looks, the giant explained, "My master will never hear."

Ah'llum taunted him with a sarcastic question: "Didn't the rabble fill our ears with the legend of his rebirth?"

"My master hears when he wants to; he doesn't hear when he doesn't want to."

"What are you saying, wretch?"

"My master hears what he wants to hear. He doesn't hear what he does not want to hear!"

"Have you seen, wretch, any creature under the moon who doesn't want to hear one day that the fates have smiled, finally, and seated him on the throne of leadership?"

"Actually, I know nothing of the nature of creatures, master, because I'm a slave who thinks with his hands not his head. But I can convey to my master the council's offer, if the lords of the council agree."

"What are you saying, wretch?"

"I'm saying that my master's secret lies in his eyes not his ears."

He put a hand in his breast pocket and drew out a highly polished stone tablet. He thrust his other hand into his tunic pocket and extracted a long piece of charcoal, as smooth as if it had been trimmed by a dagger's blade. With this charcoal he drew letters of the ancient alphabet on the polished surface. Then he knelt facing his master and raised the tablet to his eyes.

The nobles watched this cunning strategist's movement with curiosity. They observed the stillness that settled over the venerable elder for a moment but that did not last long, because his eyes suddenly narrowed, and his scrawny body responded with a tremor that did not continue any length of time, although the look from his wretched eyes afterward was not one the noblemen would ever be able to forget. Did it express astonishment, suffering, disdain, or genuine torment? Or, was it a mixture of all of these?

What the nobles remembered was that Emmamma took a handful of dirt and threw it in his poor mamluk's face as a sign of disgust. Then he drew the upper portion of his veil down over his eyes, shielding them entirely, and released a feverish gasp like his last breath, before stretching out on his back in the litter and pounding his palms on the poles as a signal to depart.

6

Before the oasis witnessed the birth of a new dawn, before the full moon came out that night, and before the council meeting adjourned that day, a messenger came to the sanctuary.

He stood in the darkness at the entrance, clenching his rough fingers together and shaking like a man with a fever.

The noblemen struggled by light from the hearth's flames to distinguish the specter's identity, and only made out the black giant after a lengthy effort. The giant spoke with the voice of a diviner conveying a prophecy to the people: "Our master has preceded us!"

Stillness settled over the place. Stillness settled over the place and proceeded to dominate every cranny of the room, the whole temple, the oasis, the wasteland beyond, and the desert—for which no one knew the beginning and no one perceived the end.

The stillness extended further, and the sticks of firewood ceased complaining as they burned in the fire's flame. The tongues of flame ceased their turmoil, which normally expressed their delight with the sticks of firewood. Chuckles died in the chests of the riffraff in the alleys. Women stopped whispering slanders and rumors, and children swallowed their rowdy shouts. The indecipherable murmurs vanished from the lips of babes in arms. The livestock stopped chewing their cud and listened despondently as their bodies turned into ears.

At that hour, the lords of the people heard news like a prophecy that was repeated by the tongue of the Unknown: "Our master has preceded us."

Finally they exchanged dumbfounded looks. After some time they discovered that the specter had vanished and that darkness threatened the place. So they fed the fire more wood.

A voice ended the long silence: "This is an evil omen!"

This voice sounded to them like another prophecy. They did not know who among them had delivered this prophecy, because they had wandered far away and their fugues lasted a long time.

The unidentified voice returned to say with the tongue of the Unknown: "The disappearance of venerable elders is always a harbinger of evil!"

Without raising his eyes from the tongues of fire, the man with two veils said: "The death of the sage forces people to discern a prophecy in his disappearance. Here he is saying to us that the honorable man prefers to lie down beside his ancestors rather than mount the world's thrones."

Someone spoke who never spoke. Someone spoke who spoke only in times of disaster. Amasis the Younger said: "We killed him. We killed the man in whom we saw the pious ancestors reflected. We found in his face the faces of our forefathers. We have killed our pious ancestors. We have killed the Law. We killed him just as we killed Aggulli before him!"

The prophetic voice rose again to swallow every other voice in the sanctuary: "The venerable elder does not disappear into the earth without a disaster descending on it."

They thrust their hands into the dirt to ward off misfortunes and to seek refuge in the earth from the evils of the people of the earth.

THE PROPHECY

1

"Our only option is to appeal for guidance to the Unknown and to place in the hand of the Spirit World what belongs to the Spirit World."

The chief merchant detected questioning looks in his companions' eyes. So this clever strategist was obliged to leave allusion's corridors in order to reach their minds.

"If the scion of the wasteland cannot deal with a matter, the riddle is transferred to the offspring of the Spirit World."

The look of inquiry remained unchanged in his comrades' eyes. Then the scion of clever strategists was compelled to descend reluctantly to the plain of clear expression.

"Our only choice is to refer the matter to the tomb maiden."

Ah'llum was the first to applaud. "Why didn't we think of this before? How could we have forgotten the presence of this diviner in our community all this time?"

But Imaswan ignored this happy news and challenged his comrade in hopes of perceiving the insight hidden in the allusion. "In the Law of our forefathers we have inherited nary a maxim that asserts a link between leadership and prophecy."

The man with two veils cast him a patronizing look and proceeded deliberately with the approach of clever strategists. He fiddled with his hands before he replied, "I see you have forgotten in a short time what we said once about the typical nature of sovereignty."

"The typical nature of sovereignty?"

"Didn't we agree that the jinn take possession of the master of sovereignty at the very hour he is seated on the throne of leadership? Didn't we agree that the head of state leaves the wasteland and loses his link to the people and language of the wasteland—to become a puppet in the hands of the residents of the Spirit World the instant he receives this noble title? Didn't our peer Aggulli serve as an example and test case for this? So how can the deity of coincidences and fortunes not rule over both of them? How can the Spirit World not be a homeland for a person who is possessed by the Spirit World, which has been an oasis for prophecy and the world's fortunes since the desert learned about prophecies and fortunes?"

"If we place the matter in the palm of prophecy, we will have entrusted our necks to the hand of luck."

"Prophecy is the tongue of the Spirit World, and where leadership is concerned, the Spirit World reigns."

"Whenever I hear the word 'luck,' I get goose bumps all over."

"Luck's dominance derives from the Spirit World's. This is the secret reason for our fear of luck's caprices."

"We have read in the narratives of the ancients that this ignoble being gives today with the right hand only when it is sure it will repossess its boons on the morrow with both left and right hands."

"The messenger isn't blamed for whatever evil lies in the message, and luck is a loyal slave of sovereignty."

"The tribes assume this is simply one of the avatars of ignoble Wantahet. Yes, yes, you should believe that luck is Wantahet."

"The desert's ultimate strategist likes to bring tribes good news too."

"But we know that glad tidings in his mouth entail a net loss. You bask in delight today and find yourself at the bottom of the abyss tomorrow."

"We must accept the abyss if our fall into it has been willed by the Spirit World."

"If the matter pertains to the Spirit World, all I can do is clasp my hands behind my back as a sign of submission."

"So we finally agree."

2

Prophecy!

Inspiration sparked by a flint of the Unknown.

Prophecy!

Panacea from the spiritual lands, it treats patients who suffer from pangs of separation, longing, and the desolation of desert lands.

Prophecy!

Heaven's tongue that yearns to speak but that communicates solely through symbols.

Prophecy!

Refuge of diviners in their struggle with the world's vanities and the fates' cruelties.

Prophecy!

The dream of poets and the hope of women singers during the tribe's soirées, when the full moon rises to reign in the desert sky.

Prophecy!

The treasure of lovers who embrace despair because death has robbed them of any hope of a tryst.

Prophecy!

A dew drop on a retem blossom, a violet glow before daybreak, a gust of sea breeze bathed in the moisture of clouds from the far north.

How can a person find the way to the Pleiades, which served as a guide, a call, a promise, and a draught of water for the ancient wanderer?

3

"*Eygahan wattmmaghan taghzzit àd sirdin addunat dagh àman en sarian; às tenkaram tegmiam talgha dagh sagheran.* Prophecy does not descend to a plain unless its inhabitants cleanse themselves with the water of solitude. Once you have finished, solve the riddle with sticks."

The messenger from the female diviner placed the scrap of leather inscribed with this prophecy in their hands. Then they found themselves pawns to a gloomy silence that reminded them of the silence they had experienced when another messenger had come to inform them of the departure of the man they had chosen from among them as their puppet. He, however, had refused to play this game and had preferred to withdraw from a realm he had always considered nugatory. On that day, his obituary had been another prophecy that had terrified the desert, paralyzed all creatures, and changed the nature of things. Today's silence, though, pervaded the council but did not affect creatures beyond their circle, for council members heard, over their silence, the bleating of goats returning from the pastures, the shouts of the herdsmen, the clamor of boys in the alleys near the sanctuary, and the cries of caravan traders in the commercial markets.

The commotion outside doubled the cruelty of the stillness inside the council chamber, but stillness is always washed with water from the heavenly spring of the Unknown and holiness. From ancient times it has been a forthright opponent of sophists who boast about the intellect's authority, because stillness has never acknowledged any union save with strangers who flee to the homelands of solitude. For this reason, people of the nugatory feel embarrassed when silence lasts a long time, because it lays bare their hidden cowardice, which they wish to camouflage and hide—even from themselves.

For this reason, perhaps, they mumbled, cleared their throats, and pretended to cough. For this reason, perhaps, the chief merchant resorted to the use of his tongue. "Obtaining a prophecy is always easier than interpreting it."

The rebel jinni commonly known as the tongue had escaped from its flask, and the pillars of silence were shaken. Then sanctity fled to the most distant land. Imaswan took heart and supported his fellow council member with the enthusiasm of a person who had been forced to refrain from speaking for a long time. "The danger of a prophecy is when its good news becomes destructive thanks to a flawed interpretation. So beware!"

The hero also attacked from his corner. "It would be best for us to take a lot of time to consider this if we wish to avoid ruin."

Imaswan seconded him by releasing the muscle that does not confirm or corroborate: "A person who disdains the exegesis of prophecy is like someone who deliberately provokes a viper." Silence returned to the chamber, but sanctity—the being that had fled to the most distant land once stillness was slaughtered—would never return.

Then people heard from the tongue of someone who normally did not speak. At that time the voice of Amasis the Younger, who was known for being taciturn, burst from his corner. "We won't obtain a trustworthy interpretation of the Spirit World's prophecy until we follow the path of the ancients."

Their curious, inquisitive looks preyed on his eyes. Then the man with two veils turned toward him to take charge. "How did the ancients do exegesis?"

"Isn't it said that they retired to the pastures and sought refuge in caverns and in deserted acres whenever they wished to proceed with any weighty matter?"

The chief merchant looked round at the eyes of the council members, who seemed as astonished as he was. Then he gazed at the eyes of the speaker, as if seeing him for the first time. He declared, "I acknowledge that this reading had never occurred to me. Doesn't this idea provide the key to interpreting the first section of the allusive statement?"

Imaswan repeated the first half of the prophecy like a poet chanting verses of poetry. Ah'llum, without meaning to, repeated it as a refrain after him. The man with two veils, however, silenced them with a new prophecy: "We must head to the grazing lands. Prepare to depart tomorrow."

The hero asked with astonishment, "But what about the second part?"

The man with two veils jumped to his feet and replied, "Solitude brings another prophecy!"

4

In the solitude of the pastures the Spirit World returns from the labyrinth to dwell in stillness. Then babbling confusion escapes from souls to satisfy their thirst by fleeing to realms that within their fortresses shelter bazaars where creatures' desires and the fortunes of the physical world loiter. So the desert steps aside with the wayfarer to give him the good news that has always been a secret with which wanderers in the desert homeland have been enamored: "All corners deceive you when they tell you that you are a transitory creature. I differ from the Law of the spiritual lands and tell you that you are an immortal creature—immortal, immortal."

Every corner, every void, every empty space, every rock, every height, every tree, every bird, every mirage, and every song of silence brings man the good news of immortality in the world of the desert. So only a minority know that solitude's splendor derives from this and that the obscure delight sorcerers call happiness comes from the loins of a glad tiding the tongue cannot communicate. Then the deluge intensifies, and those people find themselves captives of an ecstasy they had never previously experienced—not even when their ears were assailed by songs of yearning. So they released shouts of madness and approval, intoxicated by the voices of the girls singing and astonished by the vision that glowed in the sparks of longing.

In the emptiness of solitude, the council members separated and the desert tempted them with the magic of silence. So the first of them climbed a nearby hill to visit a massive tomb, which resembled a barren stone slab, because foreign adventurers had profaned its sacred space and excavated the tomb to search for treasures. The second man crept into the barren land to the north. There a mirage seized him and led him a long way into the labyrinth before casting him into a pit that rains over the years had filled with clay ripples and dirt buckles that hid truffles. The third man strolled down the trail to the south, and solitude tempted him with road dreams. So he went a long way and reached the foothills of the blue mountain chain, where he lingered on the slopes, struggled past boulders, peeked into caverns, and visited the dwellings of the jinn as an invited guest with whom they shared treasures. Then he spent an entire day touring the cave walls to experience the life of the first people through their rock art. The fourth man headed west and climbed the heights, descended onto the plains, traversed austere expanses strewn with gray stones that had been burned by the lava of volcanoes and the eternal fires of the suns. Then he perceived in the distance a camel that herdsmen had lost. She was trailed by startled newborn calves. Braying around her were camel studs expectorating the froth of their rut and extruding from their mouths *dulla* faucial bags the size of water skins. So he approached her swollen udder like a calf, thrust his head between her thighs, and seized the teat to nurse from her milk.

5

Amasis the Younger shouted in an unfamiliar voice, "The key! I think I've found the key."

The members of the council stared at him while pressing into a circle, seeking refuge near the fire from the evening chill and pretending to catch tongues of flames between their palms the way boys do. Curiosity gnawed at them, but the pride of the noblemen prevented them from uttering a question.

Their comrade stood above them, groaned from exhaustion, and bared his forearms, which he thrust into the flames as if he had decided to add them to the fire. He pulled them back deftly once he had absorbed some heat. He explained, "The second line is the key. Or—have you forgotten that we have buried seven moons and seven suns in this place for no other reason than to bicker about prophecy?"

They drew back, retreating en masse as if repulsed by food after tasting only a bite or two. It seemed that the word "prophecy" awakened in them the ancient gravitas that the desert's emptiness had pilfered from them. They had neglected to pay attention, had forgotten, had rushed off to rove around, raced each other, wrestled with one another, snatched pieces of bread and dates from each other like young men, and shouted back and forth the way slaves and herders do.

News of the prophecy awakened the ghoul of gravitas and with one blow cast them into the fetters that restrain rulers. Amasis, however, showed them no mercy. He raised his eyes to the horizon, which was flooded by twilight rays, and repeated the second line as if singing a plaintive ballad: "Once you have finished, solve the riddle with sticks."

Darkness continued to advance on the western horizon. Then moisture, perhaps tears, gleamed in his eyes. He said with a soothsayer's intonation, "In the ancient tongue, the first peoples called casting lots 'sticks.' Have you forgotten?"

They exchanged a supercilious look. Afterward they fled to the wasteland, to a stern, barren wasteland that shot off to eternity in every direction, strewn with gray rocks of extreme severity. In the distance loomed a lone acacia tree, which looked depressing in the labyrinth's desolation and—by its very existence—made the labyrinth all the crueler and sterner.

But the evening turned the matter head over heels and converted the sky into a desert and the desert into a sky. Darkness slipped down to spoil the beauty of the horizon. In the plaza of the heights, another nakedness was born and stars began to raid it. In its precincts, stars and spheres began to call back and forth to each other with allusive winks, as if eager to divulge a fear that the sovereignty of the lights might take them by surprise and erase their glow when the moon rose. A seditious charm was born in the upper desert while the lower desert died for the time being.

Imaswan objected, "Do you want us to cast lots to see which one of us will be conducted to the ghoul's corral?"

But the chief merchant could no longer bear the inspiration patiently. So he crept forward till he almost stuck his knee into the fire. He shouted zealously, "Wait! I think Amasis is onto something. 'Sticks' in soothsayers' jargon really means casting lots, because our ancestors only knew how to cast lots with sticks, but the prophecy that directed us to leave the matter to chance did not place us in the pool of candidates."

The hero broke in: "What do you mean?"

"Sticks are a method of casting lots and therefore a game supervised by a god named Luck."

"What are you saying?"

"The god of sovereignty is the Spirit World, and its partner is Luck. Luck and sovereignty share a homeland. What alternative do we have to commissioning Luck to bring us a comrade who is his neighbor in the Spirit World?"

Ah'llum looked around anxiously at his comrades. The man with two veils explained, "Games of chance have many aspects, but the ones farthest removed from calamities are the path our ancestors chose and what they preferred over all others."

They held their breath, extended their necks, and waited for more information with greater concern than if awaiting a prophecy.

The man with two veils raked the fire with a poker and added with a sage's cool detachment, "When a matter puzzled them and no inspiration came, they bathed with herbal salves, sacrificed a chameleon, and rushed off to choose the first man they met in the wilderness to be their ruler."

He was silent for a long time, gazing at the fire. Then he said mysteriously, "We'll set off tomorrow and bestow the title of leader on the first creature we meet inside the walls of the oasis!"

THE SCARECROW

1

They reached the oasis at dusk but did not breach the walls or traverse the Western Hammada Gate till sunset's gloom had mastered the earth. Then they crept through the land, which was enveloped in threadbare darkness that was not concentrated in tenebrous recesses but remained mysterious, excited whispered enticements in weak souls, and opened a portal to the nether reaches, which released a morose creature disguised in human raiment to lay a trap for mankind. The Spirit World's foot soldiers rallied their allies to form legions of armies to combat the people of the wasteland and take revenge for their tyranny. These legions returned to their homes in the Spirit World bearing booty and loot. Simpletons—people who had never ever suspected that other creatures might share the desert world—simply assumed, however, that their tribe had been attacked in a treacherous raid by some neighboring tribe. The pious ancestors were also pleased to emerge in the dark gloom from their spiritual world. They disguised themselves in the rough attire of wayfarers before visiting their descendants in this or that hamlet, where their offspring whiled away the night entertaining them the way desert people honor travelers, till morning drew nigh and light threatened to assail the wasteland just as drowsiness was assailing their hosts. Then the guests slipped away and melted into the open countryside, leaving their descendants some treasures stuffed into a knapsack.

In the tenebrous depths' void, other night creatures materialized, but they deliberately chose their former bodies to terrorize their relatives. They emerged to frighten and harm their former enemies.

In these dark recesses Wantahet awoke to devise the project of the eternal ruse. He, however, unlike all the dark recesses' other denizens, waited till day to accost the tribes—the better to deceive them.

In the desert gloom, creatures were generated in people's souls—creatures those people did not recognize. Then with all the impetuousness of ecstatics, they liberated themselves from their souls, which they pawned to other people in order to gull them of their souls and to downplay their own disgrace, referring to this sacrificial offering as "passion."

In the gloom of the barren continent, inanimate objects exchanged roles and beings migrated to the bodies of other creatures. Then the desert itself migrated from the desert's patch of ground.

On nights when no moon was visible and lights were slow to appear, cunning strategists were cautious at crossroads, because they knew from experience that talking to strangers after dusk is a danger that always risks being a trap, an evil, or a snare.

2

They hovered around him like jinni specters, addressing him with incantations. The first shouted as if performing a sorrowful ballad, "We, master, are a people who have been unable to select a head of state. Therefore we have entrusted the affair to its master, to the entity we refer to in our stupid language as a Spirit World."

The second sang, "We obeyed the report that eternity sent us as a prophecy. So we set forth, rolled in the dust of emptiness, and washed our hearts with separation's water. Then we were told that our only recourse lay in following the example of our ancestors."

The third sprang aside and then leaped with a gracious bound that mimicked an avian dance and perhaps also the ecstasy of folks who are obsessed by longing and who go into a trance when people sing. He recited, "We have come to entrust the matter to destiny's hand. We have come to court danger!"

The fourth specter shot off, fleeing toward the right for a long distance. Then he returned only to flee to the left for a longer distance. On both laps, darkness swallowed him. All the same, he returned from the Spirit World with a talisman: "You, master, from today forward are the master of this oasis. May all the nooks hear the news and may the Spirit World bear witness that we have conveyed the prophecy."

Stillness descended on the area, and the mysterious being returned from his exile to govern the oasis. Then the creatures restrained their tongues so they could eavesdrop on this creature's whispers in a pantomime of lost time. The detestable guffaws, the lethal laughter, and the suppressed cackling that people of the oasis had often heard when they passed the scarecrow in the fields and that they glossed as the voice of the Unknown—this mysterious, mischievous rattle—immediately burst from the chest of the twilight specter. Then the stillness was at once shaken, and the place became chaotic. The mysterious being, whom people had known but never seen, fled and settled in the farthest corner of the austere tract spread beneath the moon.

3

In the oasis, griots and gossips have related the story of the scarecrow. They said that an alien migrant sorcerer, when he came from the Unknown and settled in the oasis, disguised himself in rough haircloth—as members of this coterie always like to do. Then he claimed he was a metalsmith whose specialties were using metal tools to carve poles, saw planks, and turn trees into saddles. Not long after the new immigrant rented a workshop in the metalsmiths' market, residents became convinced that the man's boast was not only accurate but that he was even being modest, because his saddles differed from any they knew in markets in the oases or had purchased from blacksmith shops. His were unique for their captivating carving. People had also never seen any as skillfully crafted. Thus his renown spread in a short time, and the oasis's nobles—who had never lost their yearning for the traditions of mounted warriors—and other real cavaliers, who were leaders of tribes scattered through neighboring deserts, headed to his workshop. Traders from passing caravans also flocked to his door to buy all the saddles he had in stock. Then the merchants carried them to the deserts of the South and the cities of the North. So the cunning artisan offered evidence to slothful tribesmen and slugabeds of the oasis that anyone who perfected a task while alive would inevitably be rewarded by the Spirit World, which would convey his fame to the farthest corners.

The secret behind the smith's renown among far-flung peoples was his expertise, but it was a different story inside the oasis walls. Clever men have long realized that there is no honor for a soothsayer or diviner in a land where people do not recognize prophecy and that a product does not succeed in a land where local people view it dismissively or disdainfully. So if merchants and mounted warriors from neighboring tribes had not purchased the clever artisan's saddles, the man would not have enjoyed any share of the respect he deserved. Indeed the market for his products would have remained tepid for a long time in a land where people hid their past and piled their old saddles in the corners of their houses, allowing them to be destroyed by moths and grit. They had also traded in their purebred Mahri camels (on which tribes prided themselves, celebrating them in poems) for matted, morose, behemoth camels with bodies like an elephant—beasts fit only for transporting heavy loads.

But communities also knew that anyone who was loved by the Spirit World and who harbored its secret inside him would inevitably succeed in a pursuit—even if he lost in some other one he had perfected for the public good when people did not acknowledge his skill.

4

A captivating widow, whose beloved husband died on a business trip to the forestlands, was said to have inspired the sorcerer to construct that abominable scarecrow. She had gone into mourning, secluded herself, and rejected suitors and prospective husbands. She lived alone in the oasis, occupying her time with crooning plaintive ballads and supervising the herd of livestock she had inherited from her deceased lord.

This herd was devastated by a calamity that led her to the metalsmiths' market, where she fell under the influence of the sorcerer.

It was said that she claimed at first she thought some epidemic had infected her livestock. Wise herdsmen, however, informed her that the calamity was caused not by some mysterious epidemic but by the ravages of the vermin that creep across the face of the wasteland. She consulted a clairvoyant, who confirmed that the Spirit World was not responsible for this bloodshed. He spoke cryptically about evil intentions and concluded that the crime demonstrated the existence of a culprit. So she proceeded to set up scary figures around her livestock's corral to frighten away wild beasts. These resembled the effigies that farmers set up in their fields to scare away birds but did not save her herd from destruction. Every morning she would discover the disappearance of one or two head of livestock overnight. Outside the palm-stalk fence she would find the remaining vestiges of this nocturnal bloodbath. There were pools of blood that the dirt had absorbed till it hardened and coagulated and skeletons with their bones stripped clean of flesh with alarming efficiency—as if it had been trimmed off with a knife. Intestines were strewn about—split open and begrimed with dirt and pebbles—as digestive juices spilled from them, mixed with cud. The skins had been flayed from the body and cut into many pieces as if the perpetrator had intentionally destroyed them to ward off suspicion and to destroy the traces of his heinous deed.

At first suspicions centered on wild beasts. Many people told her that the gully the spring's waters had created at the base of the eastern section of the city wall frequently attracted reptiles, vermin, and wild beasts from the wasteland and that it was certainly not out of the question that dieb jackals had slipped in from there too. When she asked why jackals would prefer her animals to the herds of other people, they ignored this question and claimed this aspect of the mystery pertained exclusively to the Spirit World, because creatures like jackals held no grudge against her and did not descend on the oasis to slay one person's livestock instead of another's—except to deliver a message. She would need to appease the Spirit World with sacrificial offerings if she wanted to save herself and her flocks from this calamity.

The poor woman hurried to the temple and slaughtered a ewe on the tomb's threshold, but the ghoul attacked the corral that same night and slew two of the nanny goats that gave the most bountiful amounts of milk. So she despaired. She despaired without knowing that despair is the only amulet capable of conquering every calamity.

She despaired, and her despair led her to the scion of the foreigners. In the oasis they said he practiced saddle making only as a cover for the dread craft that arrogant people typically conceal whenever they migrate from their homelands. This tactician would not have succeeded in his carpentry and in fashioning poles had it not been for his mastery of that other craft—from which tribes were never secure because veils of mystery always encompassed it; its masters practiced deferential rites and demonstrated their apprehension and wariness many times.

On that day, the widow heard a boast of the type that flows from the mouths of migrants.

It is said that, after hearing the beautiful woman's recital, the clever artisan offered, "With my own hands I will build you a scarecrow unlike any ever seen in the oases. I shall give my lady an idol so sacred that not even flies will dare approach it—if my lady will allow me to carry her to the fields in my arms and carry her back as well."

At first the belle did not understand what he meant by saying he would "carry her to the fields" in his arms. She suspected the matter was some sort of joke that foreigners enjoy or an innocent caprice that citizens encounter in the conduct of artisans and that the tribes know in the eccentricities of poets. She was offended, however, and bolted away after doubt whispered in her breast and she grasped the hidden meaning of this allusion. She confided his offer to her girlfriends, who winked at each other, laughed, mocked her, and told their grannies who then asked her, "What's the harm in that? Will a man do something to a woman she does not want—even if he is alone with her in the fields? Fool, you should realize that the fool we call 'man' is merely a puppet that only does with a woman what the woman wants. Which is the lesser of the two evils: letting your herds be destroyed when their destruction entails your own, or going to the fields to play with a doll called 'man'?"

The beautiful woman hesitated for a time, but her hesitation did not last long because the nightly massacres of her flocks drove her to the cunning artisan.

5

Once the scarecrow was erected in the fields to guard over the herd's corral, the unidentified enemy vanished.

The enemy did not merely vanish; people were astounded to find a rascal's corpse stretched out beside the corral a few days later. On the slain man's neck they found blue marks that clearly showed the wretch had been strangled. Then they spread a rumor that this scarecrow differed from all the others, because it had a real creature hidden inside it. Some went even further and contended that this august body contained the person of the sorcerer himself, who had constructed this fearsome puppet with wooden poles that he clad with camel skin. Finally he stretched strips of fabric and scraps of linen over the hollow body. Then, as darkness fell, the despicable man glided through the twilight gloom to enter his vile hideout, where he spent the night, to emerge at dawn and slip back to his workshop. Others said that slaughtering the entire herd was merely a sorcerer's trick the astute artisan had used to conquer the poor widow, with whom he had fallen in love the first day. Her livestock corral had seemed the best way to win her, because sorcerers know better than anyone else that a person's heart is a pawn of his wealth and that a creature's weak point is what he possesses. When spiteful people pointed out the scarecrow's true nature in hopes of smoking out the cunning strategist, they were surprised to hear him say, "The scarecrow is twofold. One scarecrow frightens away the wasteland's beasts and predatory birds. The second terrifies human jackals, who would not be scared if it weren't the real thing." Then he released an evil laugh, which was muffled and as hoarse as the rattle of a man choking or the hiss of a serpent. This was the laugh they heard repeatedly from the mouth of his detestable dummy once it was erected in an empty place in the fields.

Sages, trying to be fair to this ignoble man, said that the scion of strangers had not wished to cause any harm, for if his work had not been beneficial, he would not have freed the oasis from the evil of the rascal whose body was dumped at the feet of the scarecrow when it was first erected. Mean-spirited men, however, considered this action a crime of the most repulsive sort and asserted that, since the damn rotter had feared he might be discovered, he had tempted to the site an innocent fool, whom he had killed with his own hands to provide people evidence of the culprit's existence (to which the seer had alluded), and to dispel doubts concerning his own plot.

If narrators differed about the circumstances of the puppet's erection and the puppet master's intentions, they agreed that the specter who emerged to meet the Council of Elders on that ill-omened evening was none other than the scarecrow from the fields. They offered as evidence the disappearance of the sorcerer of the Unknown from his workshop and the fact that no one saw him in the oasis thereafter.

THE GIFTS

1

"Here are the rewards from Luck's ally for the good opinion that Luck's emissaries hold of him."

He touched the bulging leather bag, which was decorated with magical designs, and held it up toward the elders' faces as his eyes glinted mischievously. Then he added, "Don't belittle its size, because within it you will find everything you desire!"

The council members exchanged a look that combined doubt, astonishment, and disparagement. The chief merchant protested, "Our master compensates us for our good opinion of him with a gift that shows his poor opinion of us."

"Poor opinion?"

"Does our master think we are ascetics to whom he can fling a paltry pouch and then say we'll find everything we want inside it?"

The new governor rubbed his dark hands together. Then he pulled an intensely black veil around his protruding cheeks as a nasty smile gleamed in his eyes. With the chilly hauteur of residents of the Spirit World descending to the tribes' hamlets dressed as wayfarers, he retorted, "I still feel certain that each hand will find in my modest pouch everything the soul desires."

"Does our master know that the soul desires more than the hand can reach? Does our master realize that the soul desires whatever the eye sees and that even this does not satisfy it? Then it also craves whatever it creates for itself in the imagination."

"I know. Trust me: I know."

"Then are you still certain that your knapsack can satisfy the greed of a soul that only dirt ultimately fills?"

The enigmatic smile flickered in his eyes again, and he said with great conviction, "The gifts in my little pouch will cure souls of greed and feed nations gold dust, not dirt."

A laugh escaped from the chief merchant's mouth. He laughed like a hooligan till he leaned back and his veil slipped from his mouth. Then his comrades observed depressingly black teeth in that cavity. He sat up straight and tightened the veil around his nose before asking, "Does our master wish to persuade us that all the treasures that the residents of the Spirit World have accumulated down through the ages and hidden in unknown reaches of the desert reside inside it?"

"If our venerable companion desires treasures, I will produce treasures for him from the knapsack."

"But I'm the chief merchant of this oasis and won't be satisfied, master, with a trinket."

"I wager that the chief merchant of the oasis will find a gift in the pouch that is fit for the chief merchant of the grandest oases."

"I am astonished to hear in my master's speech a certitude that puts to shame any I have ever heard from a man's mouth."

"A wise head doesn't look disdainfully at anything, no matter how trifling it appears to the eye."

"Now we are hearing the language of the Spirit World's residents who visit our dwellings camouflaged with the clothing of travelers."

"Hasn't the time come for us to discover what these souls desire so we can finally complete this task?"

The chief merchant looked round at his companions' faces. In his eyes they read a challenge, a call to arms, and a thirst for sport. So he turned back to their mysterious companion, around whose neck the fates had hung the title "leader." As if reading from an inscription burned with hot iron onto a square of leather, he said, "My longstanding dream has been to fasten around my waist a gold belt. Should I hope to find in my master's quiver a gift of gold dust fashioned into a belt?"

He leveled a derisive look at the leader and then turned toward his comrades, in whose eyes he observed a supercilious expression. The leader's eyes, however, acquired the merry look his companions had only witnessed previously in the eyes of adversaries who wait patiently to strike. He patted the leather—which was stamped with amulets—and then stuck his other hand into the mouth of the satchel, from which he extracted an object wrapped in a piece of faded dark linen. Placing the package on his lap, he untied it with the slow deliberation of a person enjoying his task. Finally he reached the item, seized the end of it the way a hunter grabs a rabbit by its tail, and held it up. Then a parlous glint ignited in thin air, and the group saw a gold belt as wide as a knuckle. It was fabricated from very minute pieces the daintiness of which added to the belt's charm and extraordinary allure. The pieces were arranged vertically in delicate links and spread out horizontally with pieces that were even smaller but all the more captivating.

The hand remained lifted in space for a long time, and the enchanting body continued to dangle in the air, where it inflamed souls with greed, desire, confusion, and insanity. Finally his palm moved to present the gift to its recipient. The leader placed the noble tail in the chief merchant's lap, releasing it slowly and allowing the gold to flow onto the seated man's lap, where it coiled up like a serpent.

Their eyes gazed at the coil with bedazzlement, awe, and astonishment.

2

Generations have discussed gift-giving, saying a gift that proves fatal if it falls below the mark becomes even more lethal if it exceeds the mark. They have related in the language of the ancients how gifts—in the first instance—generate scorn, and how they—in the second—are the lasso of subjugation that wraps around the recipient's neck.

People of the desert have handed down from generation to generation a story that the first time a gift was given, it whispered in the breast of the recipient, who was obsessed with malice and deceitful thoughts all night long. Then he found no way to doze off. So he slipped into the darkness before dawn, entered the home of his benefactor, and stabbed him with a fatal dagger blow to the heart. In the morning he went out to boast to everyone that he had taken revenge. Inquisitive people asked why he felt no gratitude for the benefaction. Then he shouted at people as loudly as he could, "Nothing in the desert so deserves punishment as a gift, because no one has the right to despise his neighbor. No one has the right to pretend he has been given more possessions than his neighbor— not even if he possesses everything on the whole disc beneath the moon. Anyone who owns something should be discreet about it to the point of feeling ashamed. He should not stand up among people to boast about what his hand, which has been soiled by deceit and lies, possesses. The sovereign is not content to possess everything on earth. He goes beyond that and gains possession of other people with gifts. For this reason, a present deserves the gravest punishment, because it isn't a boon and has never been one. Instead, it is a crime that outstrips all others, because it means spitting in the face of the Spirit World even before spitting in the face of the nobleman. So beware!"

Desert people recounted another narrative about a man who received a precious gift from one of the elders. It delighted him, and he paid off his debts with it. He invested a share in commercial enterprises. Then he dispatched caravans and purchased maids and slaves, making his fortune. He lost his peace of mind, however, and was disturbed by a feeling of being indebted and of not having repaid his debt. So he went to his benefactor and bestowed a fortune on him. Then he returned home but still could not feel calm, because the whispered insinuations he heard in his heart and saw in everyone's eyes mocked him even more, telling him in an audible voice that he would never be able to repay the debt to the lender—no matter how much he gave him—because a gift is not a loan; a gift is a loan that can never be repaid. A gift, even when repaid, still remains a debt for as long as the desert stretches beneath the dome of the sky and creatures are strewn across the wasteland.

The wretch suffered from insomnia—an insomnia he had not experienced even during his years of commercial speculations and of making deals in the markets of the oases and distant cities. He suffered from insomnia, and the insinuating whispers persisted in his breast. He felt exhausted and depressed. He neglected his herds, his commerce declined, and his stocks found no market. Then he lost his close friends, his family, and even his slaves. All he had left was ill health. He suffered with his disability for a long time, until the day sparks exploded inside him. Then he went to the residence of the man who had been his benefactor, guided by an obscure inspiration to kill him by strangling him.

Since then, successive generations have considered gift-giving to be a lethal danger. One person said that it is tantamount to spitting in a person's face. Others said that since it is a debt to the jinn, no man can repay it to another man. A third faction viewed it as a cause for civil strife and a down payment on enmity. The tribes' cunning strategists repeated a cryptic characterization of it as the Spirit World's curse.

3

It is said that when the nobles accepted gifts from the cunning strategist, he told his close associates that he had only presented these gifts as a form of self-defense, because the Law of Gift-giving grants a right of revenge to conspirators who are good to people and befriend strangers with presents and gifts. When experience taught him that time inevitably reveals peoples' hidden intentions, he saw that people rush to their demise instead of waiting for the preordained sword thrust on a day when no amount of planning will help.

Gossips attributed the death of the chief merchant (who was found strangled by his gold belt) to his excessive greed and his impudent bickering with a wayfarer whose secret he did not know and whose goal he did not perceive. He had forgotten that the being who sat before him enveloped in black was a newborn delivered by the Spirit World the previous day from the loins of the twilight before he became the creature to whom they pledged fealty that day. Then the wretch met a hideous destiny that was a far cry from the wisdom people attributed to him. Indeed, it was even said that the Spirit World's emissary, who came to the oasis disguised in the garments of a wayfarer, had punished the man with two veils in the worst possible way—first and foremost to expose this arrogant man's claim to wisdom, and secondly to teach fools the proverb that says the wisdom of a person destined to annihilation is as bogus as all the trifles destined for annihilation.

Imaswan died from being stabbed by the spear—which had a shaft studded with red gemstones—he had sarcastically asked for on that ill-omened day.

Of Amasis the Younger, tongues related how a tremor had affected him at the time of the distribution. His veil had dangled around his lips, his mouth had foamed copiously, and his eyes had glittered suddenly with a strange moisture that his peers had never observed there before. His voice had quavered with genuine emotion when he exclaimed, "Truffles! Truffles! If you found truffles for me in your bag, I would give you my whole life!"

The messenger of Luck smiled in the mysterious way that almost became an identity or a metonym for him. This was a cunning smile that only strategists have perfected. Then he thrust the hand of certainty into his frightful knapsack to extract three medium, round truffles of various colors. These were marked with mysterious, cryptic indentations that might have been drawn by the hand of a sorcerer or a diviner. Clinging to them were clods of moist, fresh, dark dirt—as if the hand of the jinn had dug these treasures from the earth of the Western Hammada and brought them from that distant land to place before this man, who was a passionate connoisseur of truffles. He began to inhale the aroma of the legendary fruit. Then he muttered guttural, unintelligible sounds and swayed east and west, weeping tears of ecstasy, affliction, and longing. The next morning they found him pop-eyed and bathed in foam and saliva. His face was spotted with suspicious blue marks herbalists said appear only on the bodies of people exposed to the most virulent poisons.

The fate of the hero Ah'llum differed from those of his comrades.

On that day Ah'llum was silent for a long time. The messenger did not entice or goad him, appearing oblivious to his existence. Unlike his comrades, the hero did not ask the sultan of gifts to produce a prodigy from his wonder-sack. Finally the hero wiped his eyes with the dark scrap of cloth and said, "Master, I have learned from experience that I lose the battle whenever I desire booty. Combat, master, is my profession, but I have learned to leave the spoils and the captives to the cowards. This principle is not merely the secret of my heroism but is also the secret of my salvation. I won't deny that I am a creature who has desires like anyone else, because I have never been as passionate about anything as my health. Indeed, I admit that good health is my true love. Couldn't my master produce from his satchel a salve or some other remedy that would heal my vision?" The mysterious creature smiled enigmatically and thrust a knowing hand into his dread sack to extract a small purse of dark cloth decorated with suspicious embroidery. In the purse the hero found coal black ashes that the master of ceremonies assured him was kohl that would restore his vision's health in the wink of an eye.

But this alleged kohl blinded him instead of healing his sight.

In spite of this affliction, the hero was the only creature destined to attend the last meeting of the Council of Nobles inside the temple that day and then also to hear the herald cry as he toured the oasis the next morning: "The soul is slain only by what it desires, and man is destroyed only by what he craves."

THE EDICTS

1

Everyone finally concurred with what the elders and sages had once said—that the disappearance of justice was preordained for life in oases. These men seemed the only faction who thought they had a right to express an opinion about life in the oasis, because they had lived another life in the wasteland before time frowned on them and forced them to settle. Then they had found themselves held hostage by enclosures, buildings, and rows of stones.

The generations who were reared within the ramparts were astonished to observe wise men tremble and shed tears when the saga of the desert flowed from tongues. These youngsters did not understand the adults' secret. So they would run after them to ask, "If abandoning the desert is this painful, why don't you return?" But these afflicted people found no answer for the question, because they themselves did not know what bound them to an earth that denied and rejected them, that made them feel they were strangers and enemies while their beloved wilderness stretched before them with all its nobility, discretion, pride, submission, affection, nonchalance, and charm. They had never discovered its secret or found anything comparable to its beauty and magic or even any explanation for these qualities. So why didn't they rush off? Why didn't they go to embrace the paradise that awaited them beyond the city walls? Why didn't they pass through the city gates and cast themselves into the labyrinth of the homeland of longing?

But . . . how absurd!

How absurd! People who had settled in the oasis knew from experience that the oasis is a siren more captivating than women singers famed for their beauty, more magical than the desert from which the arts of magic are derived, and a stronger sovereign than the most recalcitrant sultans, because it holds in its hand an indomitable weapon called "seduction."

The oasis is not content merely to entice the wretched wayfarer who has lost his way. It is not satisfied with tempting thirsty people who will perish if they do not drink from its dread deluge. It also twists around the neck of anyone alighting there the lasso of a seduction that cannot be resisted or overcome, even when the forty-night period specified by the forefathers in the Law has elapsed. The traveler relinquishes his travel plans, and the wayfarer finds himself shackled by a chain a thousand cubits long. Then he despairs and hunkers down to the earth, even while suffering from remorse and weeping for the rest of his life. He does not merely weep for his loss. He does not merely weep because of his grievous sense of the treachery of the age and his abandonment of traveling, searching, and looking for the lost longing. He weeps because he has discovered the loss of the wager and the worthlessness of the swap that moved him to sell the red-hot firebrand, a firebrand from an eternal fire, to acquire humiliation from earth he thought that he owned, whereas it owned him. It not only owned him; it slew him. If it had not slain him in the vilest possible fashion, how then could he see injustice and keep quiet about it? If it had not slain him, how could he watch the masters of the earth tighten their stranglehold around the necks of the innocent and say nothing? If it had not truly slain him, how could he be content to see the powerful continue to extend their control over his neck with taxes when he tilled the earth of the fields, went to the metalsmiths' market to forge metals, or sought to support his offspring through any other profession?

Clever technocrats said the destiny of the oases was not simply the disappearance of justice or the acceptance of humiliation, but also tyranny.

"Tyranny is the poison swallowed by everyone who finds himself held hostage by the oasis," wily strategists added.

2

The head of state told the people that if he could not bring the desert to the desert lovers, he could return to the hearts of these wretches the treasure they had lost the day they lost the desert: justice.

Then he asked forthrightly whether the noblemen of the oasis had inherited their fortunes from their ancestors. With a shout like an earthquake the throng responded, "No!" Then the cunning tactician asked in the same crafty language, "Did the landlords inherit their fields from their fathers?" The corners of the oasis rocked with, "No!" Then the governor started to pepper the crowd with provocative questions that had found their way into every mind but that had never previously been voiced by anyone. "Did the wealthy emerge from their mothers' bellies as merchants and men of property?" The walls of the oasis were shaken again by "No!" The mysterious man did not pause to take a breath or to give the throng time to reflect. Instead he concluded with the zeal of someone who had long planned his offensive: "Did the lords acquire from the Spirit World a wisdom like the sagacity that tribes recognized in their leaders, thus entitling them to rule over innocents and wretches?" The area was convulsed with a "no" stronger than all the previous ones. A tumult succeeded the convulsion. Vigorous activity among the riffraff followed the hubbub. A call followed this activity. The voice of the sorcerer, however, stopped them with a more powerful call: "Is it just for people who yesterday were free men to be enslaved by what calamitous gold dust buys or by possessions acquired through clever dodges, deceit, or lies?"

A ghoul awoke in the souls of the crowds, and a demonic afreet fidgeted in the flask as it prepared to escape from its ancient cell. People shouldered each other aside and surged through the streets, alleys, and plazas. They broke into the merchants' dwellings, wrecked the doors of shops, plundered the caravan markets, seized grain and dates stored in mattamores in the fields, snatched from each other the gold jewelry they found in gentlemen's dwellings, and dug up the yards of houses in search of pieces of gold and silver coins. Many went so mad that they stripped the noblemen's wives of their jewelry and pulled the earrings from their ears.

The oasis experienced such chaos that the sages referred to it as an earthquake, because reliable sources had mentioned nothing like it in the history of the oases.

3

It had never crossed anyone's mind that taxes were sacred until the ruler of the oasis circulated his new edicts. In previous ages, people had thought taxes were an ignoble innovation concocted by heads of state and the ruling elite to ruin the affluent and to devastate the poor and people with meager incomes in order to satisfy their own greed for luxuries. Citizens began to rise respectfully when they heard the word "taxes," however, after the cunning ruler made scoffing at taxes, tax evasion, or tax fraud into capital offenses. This punishment astonished people, because they had never previously encountered this penalty in the laws of the oasis, of the desert, of neighboring tribes, or even in the legal codes of any of the other oases scattered through the desert, where it was considered an ancient certitude inherited from the laws of the first peoples that banishment is the harshest punishment—harsher even than death.

The cruel penalty in the new legal code was accompanied by a decrease in taxes for farmers, artisans, and anyone else with a limited income. To offset the losses resulting from this tax cut, duties and taxes were increased on caravan merchants in transit, wealthy people in the oasis, landowners, and goldsmiths who melted down gold dust, minted coins, and turned the metal into jewelry and decorative items. People wanting to acquire gold dust also found in the new constitution a clear text sanctioning transactions with this metal and therefore viewed the day it was promulgated as a beginning that would free their hands— which had been restrained from such transactions by the ancient Law the ancestors had bequeathed to their heirs in other times when people had different characters, souls, appetites, and goals.

Owners of gold took the new legal code as good news, despite the alarms of weak-kneed folks and the exaggerations of anxious individuals who were terrified by the tax increase. Gold's supporters circulated happily among the people, repeating a prophecy that said it was only right for the governor to raise taxes, because he knew better than anyone else that releasing the demonic afreet from captivity would bring people profits that would offset any losses the tax hike caused.

4

In the period following Aggulli's assassination, skeptics became convinced of the ability of the spiritual lands to influence the desert lands once they saw how the age mocked the betrayed leader's aides. Tayetti, for example, the leader of the attack against the calamitous metal, knocked persistently on the doors of the noblemen to ask for help—to no avail. They also saw that when Abanaban, the chief vassal, succumbed to a serious illness, not even his closest relative stopped by his house. They observed the wretched condition of Asen'fru, the miserable tax administrator, who wandered about alone after all his companions in evil and playmates in fraud renounced him, once circumstances changed and time frowned on him.

Now that the stars had shifted, the spheres had settled in inauspicious mansions, and the Spirit World had decided to turn the system upside down and to return the order of things to its ancient mansion, people who were in denial discovered that an age had passed and that another was asking permission to come. Then they saw that those individuals who had risen above the heads of creatures by some degree and had adopted the arrogance of peacocks had begun to bend and to bow their heads. Meanwhile those who had once been abased and considered weak were stretching out treacherous hands to attack their former master deceitfully and now found themselves aides, lords, and generals in the era of the new leader.

It was said that the new lords surrounded their master the day the herald toured the alleys and plazas repeating the cryptic call that spoke of souls being destroyed by what they desired. Then the chief vassal, Abanaban, said to his master, "It perplexes me, master, that the Spirit World should have destroyed upright lords and spared Ah'llum, whom Aggulli trusted more than anyone else, even though he was the first to strike the leader treacherously on that fateful day."

It was said that the mysterious emissary was silent for a long time that day and then rolled up his sleeves to reveal his dark arms—something he always enjoyed doing—and began to pursue with his eyes the early-afternoon mirage that was rushing through the open countryside. Finally he replied in a way that people thought opaque: "If we had been granted knowledge of the natural characteristics of the Spirit World, we would have the right to make rules for things. We have frequently thought that we have been afflicted by an evil only to learn quickly that the act was good for us. We have frequently seen a matter we reckoned good turn bad. So what proof do we have that those we think have gone to death and damnation have not been chosen for another destiny that we find no path in our world to attain, namely happiness? What leads you to believe that the Spirit World only keeps a person alive to inflict suffering on him?"

The group was still for a long time, and a gloomy silence prevailed. They discerned a mournful look in the master's eyes and prepared to leave. The emissary of the Spirit World, however, stopped the chief vassal, to whom he remarked, "Here's some advice for you from me. I wouldn't confide this to you if you weren't going to be my right-hand man. Don't hold a grudge for any evil. Don't gloat over the suffering of someone who harmed you one day. Remember, as well, that this is not merely a condition imposed by someone the Spirit World has chosen to rule the people, but that you must learn that the source of happiness is hidden here. So beware!"

BLINDNESS

1

Suns do not rise or set, days do not come and go, stars do not vanish because they do not appear, and the stars do not appear because the skies have fled from the heavens, and the desert has disappeared because there is no existence for a desert in a homeland in which the sky has no existence. Nights also do not fall, because night has swallowed everything and nothing exists except the night.

For the first time an earthquake struck the two immortal companions and produced the obscure fissure separating time from space, its bosom friend. Then spaces vanished from every space and swam in the dark recesses' void, where time also was stifled. Since anyone who does not find a space for himself in space does not live, anyone who ceases to exist in a space is also abandoned by time. Then he traverses the sacred Barzakh isthmus to gaze at an eternity that exists only in those tenebrous depths that blindness creates. No one knows why past generations have feared blindness so much that the forefathers considered it the ultimate punishment for malefactors, gouging out the eyes of criminals to deprive them of the enjoyment of looking at their beloved desert. They continued this tradition for long ages until an enlightened generation viewed this punishment as so cruel that it was suitable only for barbaric tribes. Then they debated with the people and discussed the matter with soothsayers, sorcerers, and leaders. So, nations enacted new laws that replaced blinding with the expulsion of criminals from the encampments and their forcible exile.

During the first period he enjoyed his exile and thought about time—which only dies in the tenebrous depths—and asked himself repeatedly about the secret of blindness, about the ability of this alleged ghoul to transform the pattern of life, about how it becomes something that people always consider worse than anything else. Yet it infuses the body with other fresh breaths and prolongs a transitory lifespan into flourishing lifetimes that the wilderness does not muddle, futile days do not sully, and visions do not confuse. Instead they evolve into a different journey that slithers forward with the elasticity of serpents, flows like the tongues of torrents down valley bottoms, and stretches to extend to an indeterminate end time. Perhaps peace of mind plays a role in this upheaval. Perhaps the key factor in this miracle is tranquility. Perhaps the reign of the dark recesses is a nodal point in space, and perhaps the disappearance of space eliminates its companion—time—from the desert. Then peace settles in the heart and confers delight in the Spirit World.

But what type of delight is achieved in the Spirit World? When was the life of the Spirit World a comrade for the life of the desert? Does someone who has lost the desert truly live when he no longer finds a space for himself in space?

2

In another time, or perhaps beyond another time—perhaps far from all times—he discovered that what he had thought was an existence beyond the desert and beyond space and time, and what he had believed to be bliss in the realm of the Spirit World, was merely the abyss of the dark recesses and the most hideous visage of blindness, and that the tribes of the first peoples had not erred when they blinded evildoers, making that their ultimate, harshest punishment. He discovered that life in the tenebrous depths is not a blessing, as he had once thought, that it is not bliss in the realms of the spiritual worlds, as he had always consoled himself, that it is not tranquility in the shade of retem trees or acacias, that it is not a life in life, because it is outside of life and man cannot be satisfied with a life outside of life—even in a paradise in the kingdom of the dead, even if he were installed as a god over life in a realm in which life did not exist. He discovered that his discounted realm did not become the neighbor of eternity simply through its liberation from the dominion of the desert lands. He discovered that his kingdom was more wretched than he had originally suspected, because its magic came from his—the hero's—liberation from the fetters of the futility with which men had always manacled him. When time afflicted him and folks pitied him for his calamity, they dropped him and shunned him. Then the only companions he found were solitude, loneliness, and the tenebrous depths of blindness. So he relaxed, reposed, and for the first time savored peace.

This torpor deceived him, enticed him, and led him far away. This daze cast him into lands he did not know and dropped him in territory he had never considered, because recluses have learned from long experience that isolation is a secret that steals a novice from his soul and that hurls a person who loves it passionately to a world that can destroy the minds of weak souls, because it is a world that can be reached without travel. The elite do not ride donkeys when searching for it, because it lies hidden in a space nearer to its master than his jugular vein.

Was his realm inspired by recluses' fantasies?

Shouldn't he call things by their true names and refer to his presumptive paradise by its true name? Wasn't the abyss of the tenebrous depths a dungeon more hideous than any other? Weren't the ancestors justified in casting evildoers into this pit, which obviated the need to build a wall or prison around anyone the fates condemned to this destiny? Finally, was darkness a deprivation of seeing the desert—as fools believed—or a deprivation of that riddle called life?

3

Just as the newborn's scream is a sign of childbirth, a genuine prophecy must be preceded by a sign.

Shortness of breath and gasps like death rattles were his first sign.

He did not recognize how, when, or why the labor pains began. What he did perceive was a vision like the inspiration of a prophecy. Sparks like a flint's shot from a location in the vast ocean of tenebrous depths. There was no flame. There was no flash of lightning, no firebrand like that preceding dawn's birth. There was, instead, an insignificant light—a depressing, faint, meager glimpse, a snuffed-out gesture lacking even a shadow to celebrate the light or to remind a person of greedy fires; but this feeble gesture lit a blaze in his breast on that day.

The blaze began the moment the spark fell into the ocean of blackness. Then it faded, waned, and almost vanished. Soon, however, it ignited in the heart a strange tingling that long before had become part of forgetfulness. The tingling proceeded to blaze, to accelerate, and to grow large enough to swallow the entire continent of dark recesses. Light flowed out, inundating every space. Then he found himself leaping naked into the air the way young boys celebrate the arrival of a cloudburst, raising his hands high to catch beams of the noble light in his palms. The heavenly deluge showered his naked breast, scoured his skin, and washed it with its rays. He was cleansed by the beams of light and imbibed this lost light like a thirsty man imbibing drops of rain after a drought. Golden strands woven from the linen of innocence, translucence, and diffidence crisscrossed to traverse the body of the creature who had no body, to transform his body into innocence, translucence, and clustered diffidence, to exchange places with the gift, to turn the light into a body, to transmute his body into a cluster of charm, translucence, and light, so he became light and that light became a creature called the hero.

But . . . but the inspiration died, and the sign soon died out.

The sign was extinguished, and so the illumination vanished.

The tenebrous darkness descended and became more tyrannical than at any prior time. He searched for the prophecy. He sought out his lost true love. Then the darkness exhaled a viper's hiss into his face. His chest constricted, and he began to choke. He gasped for breath. The fire blazed in his chest. So he leapt and roared like the forestland's lions.

He kept rubbing his eyes as mercilessly as if wishing to pluck out his eyeballs. He roared with a ferocity no one had ever experienced from him before that day.

4

His slaves came to help, assuming that their master had been stung. They gathered around him in alarm, but he kicked one of them and drove others away with his left hand. His right hand was still digging into his eye sockets in a lethal attempt to pluck out his eyes.

During this struggle, the haughty hero, who in the oasis was exemplary for his dignified conduct, screamed in a horrid voice that could only be compared to the sounds produced by prime camels when herders crouch over them to remove their testicles: "Ah . . . ah . . . ah . . . ah . . . ah . . . ah. . . ."

The hero's wife fled from their home in alarm while men, slaves, herdsmen, boys, and gawkers approached their dwelling.

Then the hero was able to escape into the alley, shaking off the slaves while continuing his lethal attempt to pluck out his eyeballs.

Abanaban, the chief vassal, arrived and went to the head of the group. He asked, "Is the man possessed?"

No one replied, because at that moment the group saw the hero seize his beloved mamluk's neck, which he gripped, and drag him along while he bounded around. The poor man began to foam at the mouth, to choke, and to rave as his eyes bulged out and his veil fell off. "Master! Master! Master!"

Someone shouted, "Watch out! The wretch will die at his hands!!"

A band of slaves rushed to save him, but the hero brushed them aside as easily as if they had been a swarm of flies and returned to his painful song, even though its secret meaning escaped them: "Ah . . . ah . . . ah . . . ah . . . ah. . . ."

The hero proceeded to hop and leap from place to place while retaining his stranglehold on his favorite slave and continuing to dig at his eyes with his other hand. Short, potbellied, and breathless, Tayetti— leader of the attack on the forbidden currency long ago—approached. He shouted as loudly as he could: "Ropes! Where are the raffia ropes? Where are the men? Where are the guards?"

As some individuals galloped off in search of ropes, he cautioned the remaining group, "Watch out! I think the wretch is dying!"

Some members of the crowd summoned their courage and rushed to save the slave, who continued to struggle to free his neck from his master's grip. Finally his powers failed him, and he went slack. He yielded, despaired, and foamed profusely at the mouth. Two large eyeballs—red with terror, astonishment, and blood—protruded from their sockets.

Some men grabbed the hero's two hands, and the demonic afreet jerked them across the earth for a short time. Then he hurled them into the void, and they flew through the air like a couple of scrawny puppets stuffed with straw.

They landed far away.

Men carrying coils of rope arrived and assailed the hero from two opposite directions, grasping their savage, twisted rope. Tayetti gave them a stern signal. So they exploded and galloped round the afreet, employing the strategy customarily used on raging camels in seasons of rut. They tightened the rope around the afreet. Then they stopped and waited for another signal. When Tayetti was slow to give one, the men stopped waiting. Screaming like madmen, they pulled the ropes right and then left in a heroic effort to topple the hero.

But the onlookers saw the group's iron men thrown to the earth, while the hero continued to run around and roar like a jungle lion.

Someone called out the desperate prophecy, "I fear the wretch has died!"

The group grumbled, and the strongmen felt desperate. Then the leader appeared.

The crowd made way for him. He advanced through the plaza in a black garment—like a crow from the badlands—and stopped only a few feet from the hero. Stillness descended on the plaza—a stillness broken only by the afreet's screams.

The leader asked sarcastically, "Instead of fetching waterskins, you send for raffia ropes?"

Tayetti approached inquisitively. Then the leader scolded him indignantly, "Don't you know that fire's enemy is water—not ropes?"

Tayetti replied like an idiot, "We actually didn't understand, master."

The leader chided him, "Put out the blaze! Bring water!"

Astonished, Tayetti retreated, and men rushed to fetch water. It was said that the hero calmed down and collapsed once people had poured two skins of water over his head, but the poor slave had been strangled by his grip.

WANTAHET

1

It is related that the hero—once he was liberated from possession by the jinn—retreated to a corner of his house and wept for his dead slave there for days. The herbalist came to treat his bloody eyes, which he had almost plucked out during his temporary insanity on that ill-omened day. He found his patient swaying side to side like a person in an ecstatic trance. His veil was dangling down, revealing the lower half of his face. From his chest rose a muffled, painful wail, and with his fist he was pounding a monotonous beat on the house floor—which was covered with skins—as if keeping time to an unknown tune no one else could hear.

The herbalist hovered around him for a time and then knelt nearby. He flung his supplies on the mat and stretched out a lean, dark hand marked with veins, creases, and old scratches, to examine the bloody eyes—even though his feverish patient never stopped pounding the hide with his mysterious beats, which he paired with a vague dance and an inaudible tune.

When he loosened the bandage wrapping the eyes, he found that the linen had adhered to the eyelids as the blood dried. Then he, too, began to sway back and forth, as if mimicking the hero, and released a long, barely audible moan. He plunged his fingers into a container filled with a dark, viscous liquid and began to anoint his patient's eyes. He continued to moan his mysterious song till he finished freeing the scrap of cloth from the dried blood. He pulled the cloth away, and then the damage to the eyes was obvious. They were bloody and swollen, as if a wild beast's fangs had ravaged them.

The herbalist scooted back and sighed deeply. He remarked like a diviner repeating a prophecy: "When a herbalist is perplexed about the cure, a patient is left with the choice between a sorcerer or a diviner."

He dipped a piece of black linen in another container, which was filled with a green liquid, and began to massage his patient's eyes with that. He added, "It doesn't harm the herbalist to acknowledge his inability to effect a cure when he sees that the malady resisting him isn't—like ordinary diseases—an enemy spawned by the wasteland, but a messenger from the Spirit World."

He tossed the rag aside and drew a leather pouch from his satchel. He untied its ribbon very slowly and sprinkled dark powder into his palm. Then he spread this suspect dust around the eyes, and the maniac responded for the first time by ceasing his muffled moaning, even though his fist continued to pound the mat with the same beat.

"I haven't concealed anything from my master. I shared my doubts with him about the affliction the first day."

The feverish hero resumed his moaning, swaying, and drumming.

The herbalist soaked another piece of cloth in a liquid from another container and then wrapped the cloth around the invalid's head.

He started to bandage the eyes carefully and remarked in the same enigmatic tone, "I wasn't stingy with advice for my master yesterday. I haven't been stingy with advice for my master today. My master would do himself a favor if he went to the diviner or sorcerer today, not tomorrow. The stubbornness of heroes, master, is useless in combatting diseases from the Spirit World."

He emitted a long, heartrending groan, and tears formed in his eyes. He traveled far away—the way lovers, hermits, wayfarers, poets, and ecstatics do. He hummed as if singing a stanza of poetry from an ancient epic.

"Physical pains afflicted man one day, and the herbalist arrived in the desert. Secret pains afflicted man one day, and the herbalist couldn't find a cure for them in the desert's herbs. So man was about to go extinct. Then the spiritual worlds collaborated and sent the sorcerer to the wasteland. When man was afflicted by other, even more mysterious diseases, and was threatened by annihilation once more, the Spirit World intervened and man found that the soothsayer had settled in the wasteland—as if he had sprouted from the belly of the dirt like grass or truffles or had fallen from the sky like rain or specters of jinn."

2

He went to visit the female diviner.

She appeared and sat with him in the Chamber of Sacrificial Offerings.

She said with a diviner's tongue: "The pains of heroes are the calamity of hypochondriacs."

"And the sympathy of noblemen is the calamity of heroes."

"I thought that the sympathy of the nobles was always a balsam."

"A balsam for the masses and for foreigners but a fatal blow to the hearts of the elite men commoners refer to as heroes."

"Are you sure about this or do you merely suspect it?"

"Actually, this is the normal course of events, my lady. We have typically grown accustomed to finding people gloating whenever calamities strike our homes."

"Enemies' gloating for the judicious man today is a treasure that will help him on the morrow."

"The matter would be easy, my lady, if this gloating was that of enemies. The gloating of boon companions, my lady, leaves an aftertaste in the throat bitterer than colocynth."

"But this is also the Law of things."

"You're right, but I don't know why we acknowledge all the laws, accepting even the harshest of them, and yet disparage the Law that makes yesterday's boon companion the first to deliver a blow when calamity strikes."

"This is the wisdom of the Spirit World."

"But this is a cruel wisdom, my lady; it is a wisdom crueler than any other."

"The Spirit World does not offer us its wisdom gratis. The Spirit World has given it to us on the understanding that we will pay the full retail price."

"But that's the cruelest possible price."

"We should trust no one."

"Tribes customarily teach this lesson to their children without understanding it."

"The phrase is brief, as you observed, but exposes our life to danger if we understand it too late."

"I don't understand wisdom's utility when understanding it too late is a precondition for it."

"True wisdom is only understood after it is too late."

"This is what's worst about the matter. This is what's worst about wisdom."

"But let's drop the question of wisdom and search for the cure."

"The truth is that my only reason for approaching the sanctuary has been to search for a cure."

"My tongue may possibly reveal something that embarrasses me."

"I will give my lady everything I possess if my lady will show me the sun's disc."

"My tongue may possibly reveal something that embarrasses me."

"I will give my lady everything. I will give her even the title 'hero,' which became part of me, if my lady can show me the sun for a single day, a single hour, or a single instant."

"My tongue may possibly reveal something that embarrasses me."

3

"In the urine of a woman who has known only her husband is found the cure."

The prophecy was inscribed on soft gazelle-skin parchment wrapped in a piece of faded linen and fastened with straps of colored leather. Her messenger brought it at twilight. He said his mistress refused to accept any fee for this prophecy until the cure was effected.

"In the urine of a woman who has known only her husband is found the cure."

What correlation does the Spirit World see between women's liquids and sorceries that blind the eye? Why does prophecy keep surprising us with one marvel after another? Or—does the secret of prophecy rest in its marvelous quality? Would prophecy lose its magic if marvel were not its mate?

But he knew better than to ask too many questions. He knew that what is covert is the Spirit World's share and that he had no right to question a matter that time had not brought to the badlands. He knew that stubborn resistance to a sign differs from a hero's stubborn resistance to enemies with spears or swords. He knew that obtaining a prophecy's text was easier than expounding it and that the exegesis of a prophecy was easier than searching for the secret behind a prophecy.

But . . . how could he find a woman in this desert who had known only her husband? In an oasis where nations mixed together, where a babel of foreign tongues was heard, where human nature was up for grabs—would he be able to locate a woman protected by the amulet of faithfulness? Would he discover anywhere in the desert even one woman who had never cheated on her husband—if not with her body surely at least in her heart? Would the Spirit World generously provide news from the Spirit World without inserting into the message an impossible condition? Didn't the Spirit World say prophetically that woman could deceive even herself—as she was always happy to do—but could not deceive the Spirit World a single time?

But. . . .

But why look so far? Why would he need to hunt far away when the creature whose chastity was discussed in poems and whose conjugal faithfulness her female companions lauded did not live in the homelands of the ancient epics, but slept beside him? Wasn't his wife the only creature whose chastity would never be doubted—not even by the dread Spirit World—after people's tongues had spoken of it and crowned her head with chastity?

4

Man's liquid caused the dispute between the sorceress and her neighbor. Ancient cautionary tales report that the sorceress heard her neighbor disparage the value of this liquid and call it polluted. So she scolded and cautioned her. But like any other chatterbox, this neighbor gave free rein to her tongue in women's gatherings and thoroughly lambasted and slandered the magical liquid. It was said that she took great delight in vilifying it and spat in disgust whenever her girlfriends mentioned it. The sorceress's patience with her neighbor was exhausted, and she decided to teach the fool a lesson that only a practitioner of sorcery can deliver. She wandered in the northern badlands by night and conversed with the heaven's stars. Lovers tarrying in the wastelands heard her loud debate with jinn demons but did not fathom the reason for the dispute till some days later when ischuria afflicted her wretched neighbor, and this human liquid was retained by her haughty body.

She closeted herself in her tent, sent out for salves and macerated herbs, and swallowed juices prescribed by grannies. She drank chamomile tea for three days straight and swallowed wormwood elixir for the next three. Then she stewed colocynth fruit and drank the broth and also consumed the seeds, but the illness was not affected, and the human liquid was retained even more stubbornly by her body. The miserable woman was obliged to descend from her high horse and to send for the herbalist.

The herbalist drew many herbs from his satchel and gave her lots of liquids to drink, but her urine retention persisted. So the woman was burning with fever and began to struggle with bouts of insanity.

Finally the herbalist admitted he could not cure her—as every desert apothecary does when he realizes that a condition's etiology is mysterious. He told the woman that herbalists were created to treat physical ills the wasteland spawns, but that wasteland inhabitants would be obliged to search for a cure for Spirit World illnesses from the masters of the Spirit World. Then the arrogant neighbor woman was forced to descend from her high horse a second time; she summoned the sorceress.

The sorceress entered her neighbor's tent and was surprised to find there—instead of her neighbor—a specter . . . a shriveled, pale, unkempt female jinni, whose large, protruding eyeballs glowed with anxiety, pain, and insanity. In her pupils was that distressing sign seen only in the eyes of people whom time has afflicted with an unexpected calamity so that they find themselves standing before the house of destruction without ever yielding to an unknown destiny or believing that death might be so easy.

The sorceress stood by her longtime neighbor's head and remarked, "What do you suppose a person in whom human liquid is retained will give if one day a person is found who can expel from the body poisoned by this pollution a single drop of the sacred liquid that purifies man from his defilements?"

The neighbor woman collapsed and howled at the top of her lungs. Wallowing in the dirt at the feet of the longtime sorceress, she begged, "A person suffering from urine retention will give everything her hand possesses to the person who can expel from her body a single drop of the one liquid that purifies man's body from man's defilement."

"I am happy to hear a tongue describe man's water as sacred today after I heard it accuse urine yesterday of all types of impurity."

"Man, my lady, is a dull-witted child who does not realize that fire burns till it scorches his fingers."

"Man won't be wise, man won't be happy, till he recognizes the contrary in its contrary."

"It is pointless to think the haughty fellow will learn that before the day he receives a punishing lesson."

"Isn't it astonishing that you described man's water yesterday as impure and today characterize it as sacred?"

"I would not have admitted that, my lady, if time had not taught me such a severe lesson."

"Know, then, that man's water is like a chameleon's saliva, which is lethal poison for vipers but the strongest antidote for sorcery in man's body."

"I have heard that the chameleon overpowers the sorceries of foreigners."

"The water that exits from the body is a secret like the chameleon's saliva. It literally kills grass because it is a herbicide, but purifies bodies of their poisons."

"No creature who exists in the desert could possibly believe my lady's statement as fervently as the miserable wretch kneeling at your feet."

"In man's water resides man's cure!"

"You're right, my lady."

"What is man's water, which fools refer to as urine? Isn't man's water life itself?"

"Man's water is life!"

5

He came to the temple escorted by two of his slaves, who seated him on the mat in the Chamber of Sacrificial Offerings. Then he ordered them to leave. Alone, he sat erect at the center of the chamber, scouting the stillness and fending off demons in the abyss of darkness. Even so, he did not hear the footsteps of the lady in the *thawb*.

He did not hear her footstep but did hear her voice. "I never expected to see the token of the disease still around the eyes of the hero of heroes after the prophecy."

"How futile!"

"I am not disappointed about losing any hope of receiving a payment for the prophecy, because the wealth of diviners is not a gift from the physical world but a prophecy from the Spirit World. What has shaken me is a husband's disillusionment with his wife's chastity."

He moaned expansively, and his fingers trembled violently. Slender fingers, which no longer resembled those that had earned him the title of hero, extended and slipped through the fuzz of the leather mat's thick hair in an attempt to stifle his emotion and to mask the trembling of his fingers.

He spoke with the nobility of the last of the nobles. "Had it not been for my longstanding confidence in it, I would have doubted the truth of prophecy."

"Is it right for a champion of the intellect to doubt the Spirit World and instead believe a woman's word?"

"I admit, my lady, that this would be inappropriate. I acknowledge to my lady that this would be sheer stupidity. But what does a man have left when he is deceived by a wife whose nobility has been discussed by the tribes and whose chastity has been celebrated in extremely beautiful verses by poets?"

"The ultimate wisdom is not to believe a woman. The ultimate wisdom is never to trust a woman."

"Was woman born to be an artiste?"

"All women are artistes. Woman is a born artiste."

"Time has slung its catastrophes at me on three occasions in one span. The first was the day we elevated above us the Spirit World's emissary, who stripped me of all my titles. The second was the day I imagined that one man could rescue another from an ailment, affliction, or any other loathsome condition and therefore accepted for my affliction medicine that blinded me and confined me to the abode of tenebrous darkness. Now time has struck me for a third time and stolen from my bedchamber a beloved whose chastity was proverbial among the tribes."

"Catastrophes refuse to descend to the campsites singly."

"We always badmouth time's treachery but do not swallow the bitterness of this treachery till time betrays us."

"Did you believe that heroism consists of withstanding the thrusts of spears or the blades of swords? Today, do you believe that true heroism means bearing the blows of the age—not those of people armed with weapons?"

"That's true. The masses puff us up with their cheap praise. Then we believe the lie and strut among people with all the arrogance of peacocks. We do not discover the fraud till the Spirit World frowns and inflicts punishment on the empty lands."

"Here, at last, you speak with the tongue of wisdom."

"But why doesn't wisdom come before it is too late?"

"This is the nature of wisdom. This is the secret of wisdom."

He was silent, and so was she. After a lengthy pause she repeated to herself, "This is the secret of wisdom."

6

The day of the confrontation, the disclosure began with a stern question. "Do you understand that a man can bear being betrayed by a bosom friend but not by a sweetheart?"

She drew the scarf around her captivating cheeks, which were draining of color and losing their beautiful complexion.

Anger overwhelmed him, immediately robbing him of a wise man's dignity. He shouted in a voice that was totally unlike any he had ever used: "I have come to hear the truth from you now."

Pallor assailed her entire face, and its beauty retreated in alarm. Worry's shadow peered from her captivating eyes. She muttered, "What do you want to hear?"

"I want to hear what must be heard."

"What's the point of hearing what you will hate to hear?"

"I want to double my pain. Perhaps the draft of poison I consume will prove poison's antidote."

She looked down at the earth. Anxiety disappeared from her eyes, where enigmatic mystery now settled.

She gazed up at him suddenly. Then mystery turned to defiance in the wink of an eye.

She spoke calmly, almost coldly. She addressed him with the composure that has always been the hallmark of the brave. "He was a wayfarer!"

"What are you saying?"

"He came as a wayfarer. So I offered him the only hospitality a woman can offer a man."

"What are you saying?"

"I told myself that the transient paradise belongs to the transient, as the Law has taught us, and that the paradise of the male transient is a woman."

"Are you lying?"

"I offered him a treasure that has always been man's safe deposit with woman!"

"If only I had lost my sense of hearing and not my sight so I wouldn't be hearing what I am now!"

"Don't think I acted this way to satisfy some caprice or in response to the desire of a woman whose husband is away. I did it as retribution!"

"Did you say 'retribution'?"

"Yes. Absolutely. A woman does not lie in the same bedchamber with another man unless she is plotting some revenge. Don't believe what is said about the phenomenon of flirtatious women."

"What revenge are you discussing?"

She shot him a spiteful glance. Looks like this escape a woman unintentionally and glow like sparks from a flint, but are immediately extinguished when the woman regains her self-control. She deleted the spiteful look and replaced it with captivating seduction when she pelted him with this cutting question: "Have you forgotten that you abducted me from my father's home?"

He lifted his hand to the cloth bandaging his eyes and grasped the piece of linen as if intending to rip it off and toss it far away. He swayed back and forth like a man in mourning. Suddenly he became still.

Then he asked, "Did I do something the first peoples didn't? Did I violate the Law we inherited from our fathers? Did I perform some foul deed when I took you from a tent that was a prison for you?"

"That tent you term a prison was my only safe nook."

"I'm amazed by what I hear."

"Know that a woman never forgives her man for taking her from her father's home."

"You speak about your father's home the way inhabitants of the desert speak about the alleged paradise."

"You may doubt whether the paradise the desert's inhabitants sing about exists, but beware of doubting the father's paradise!"

"Amazing!"

"A father's home is a nest for the virgin. If she leaves it one day, she will never return. If she leaves it one day, she loses the way back to it— and loses herself as well."

"I've never heard anything like what you're saying."

"Woman watches for opportunities for revenge, because she hasn't found the treasure they deceitfully told her she would find in man's arms—happiness!"

"Happiness?"

"This fairy tale definitely does not exist beside a man."

"I doubt that this fairy tale exists anywhere."

"Woman is the only creature who knows where this treasure is found."

"You're talking about happiness? Who can say decisively where happiness hides?"

"Man's happiness is with a woman, but a woman's exists elsewhere."

"Amazing!"

"Man's happiness is with a woman, but a woman's exists elsewhere."

7

Revenge. . . .

Revenge is a way of life in the realm of the desert. Successive generations have reported that many other advocates preceded the advocate of revenge to the desert.

The advocate of revenge was the last partisan to enter the barren land but surpassed all others in sovereignty and sorcery.

He is said to have found his predecessors embracing one another and pretending to be fond of each other by day but competing to plot conspiracies against each other once night fell. Thus the desert's very pillars rocked with their ignominy. Then the desert's inhabitants were in an uproar because of this chaos.

The cunning strategist climbed a mountain and from it spied on his rivals in sorcery. The advocate of anger darted at his companions' faces like a raging dust cloud. The advocate of envy smirked while fashioning snares behind his back. The advocate of hatred was taking advantage of his two foes' distraction while bracing to deliver his own blow with a hand held out of sight.

The advocate of revenge chuckled, then the summit trembled, and the mountain's rocks shook. This wily strategist told himself that his adversaries posed no threat to him, because they had only been provided with a limited knowledge of the science of duplicity. He characterized them out loud as playful tikes and empty puppets the winds tossed about. Then. . . .

Then the cunning strategist decided to enter the playing field to teach these fools some tricky moves.

He donned a slave's tattered rags and approached his rivals at noon, when they were hugging and pretending to like each other while performing rituals of mutual respect. He told them he was a mamluk of the leader and had come as a messenger from His Majesty to deliver an invitation to a banquet grander than any the desert had ever witnessed throughout its long history. They stared at him suspiciously at first. Then the advocate of anger darted at this messenger, demanding a sign from him. Before the wily strategist responded to this demand, the advocate of envy jumped up and pointed at the mount's bridle, which was embellished with gold galloons and set with rows of precious stones. He asked, "How could a slave have a treasure like that bridle? When have slaves ridden beasts adorned with treasures? I wager, wretch, the donkey also belongs to your master!" The wily strategist prostrated himself till his turban touched the naked land's dirt and asked reverentially, "Does a mamluk in our desert own anything besides his dreams, master?" So the fools chuckled together for a long time. Then the advocate of hatred remarked, "You're right, wretch. We're sure a slave doesn't even possess his tongue, because his master can rip it out by the roots the moment he feels angry." They guffawed together again. Then the emissary announced, "My master provided me with the gold bridle as a sign for you." Doubts dissipated in hearts that had never known anything but doubts, and these master sorcerers raced each other to attend the leader's banquet on the neighboring plain. The wily strategist seated them on a carpet of incomparable beauty, served them dishes more delicious than any people had ever tasted, and poured them a beverage so ambrosial they sang ecstatically. They became excited with desire and embraced each other according to banquet etiquette. When the wily strategist determined that the Day of Retribution had arrived, he rose to address them with a vengeful tongue for which these fools were totally unprepared.

"Does the advocate of anger recall the day he approached my tent as a traveler and I gave him shelter, fed him, and supplied him generously from my stocks? Does the advocate of blameworthy anger remember how he returned the favor before leaving my dwelling by strangling me with his bare hands after an innocent piece of advice from me awakened volcanic wrath in his breast? Advocate of envy, do you recall that I accompanied you in a caravan to the forestlands and that my commercial success there and the enthusiastic reception for my wares hurt your feelings so badly that on the way home you waited for me to fall asleep and then stabbed me with an enchanted dagger, plundered all my possessions, and fled from that place, thinking you could flee from punishment? As for you, advocate of hatred, on your behalf I repaid a major debt and freed you from the captivity of a clan determined to take you as a slave to their encampments for your failure to repay it. Then you slit my throat with your blade to reward me for my good deed. Did you fools assume that a person protected by good intentions could be harmed by a chokehold, a dagger thrust, or the slash of a sword? Cowards, don't you know that innocents don't die? Don't you know why innocent people become immortal? Listen to a secret you'll never hear again. Innocent people do not die, because they harbor in their hearts a ghoul named revenge. Innocent people do not die before they take their revenge. Innocent people do not even die if they take revenge, because revenge is the Law that prevents disorders and restores everything to equilibrium, because it is a talisman borrowed from the will of the Spirit World—not from the inhabitants of the wasteland."

The cunning strategist pulled the dread carpet out from under their bodies, and the fools fell together into a bottomless abyss.

Successive generations have said that tribes gave the name "Wantahet" to the advocate of revenge. Other communities dubbed him the "Master of Deceit." Some nations have lauded his heroism, but other lineages have satirized his wily ignobility in their epic poems. Some clans have applauded his spirit of vengeance and repeated a statement attributed to this cunning strategist that he had decided to do no evil because he was certain that the evil would inevitably turn to good, thanks to the Law of Contradictory Effect, and never to do any good, because the good would inevitably turn into evil.

It is also said that Wantahet's faith in vengeance was responsible for turning this wily strategist into an immortal being.

THE EPIDEMIC

1

The advocate of revenge does not die. Since he has embraced retribution, however, he must necessarily kill his enemies by tricking them, if he wants to avoid dying. Just as hermits disappear into distant mountain caverns, a person thirsting for revenge digs a cave for himself in a spot near the jugular vein in order to peer out at his foes. He does not lose his focus or blink, because he needs to keep his sight fixed on the rabble.

In himself he slays the man he knew, rids himself of his inborn character, and liberates himself from desires, passions, and pleasures. At first he snubs his fellow liars. Then he quickly disavows his father, mother, and child—and every other relative—in order to seclude himself with his idée fixe, which is a vision, inspiration, and whispered temptation. He begins with self-denial; he starves himself so he can dine on his dread treasure, goes thirsty so he can quench his thirst with the secret that dwells inside him, and slays his body's senses to bring to life the invisible ghoul. He ogles death and even goes to the sacrificial altar to present his life as an offering, because he knows that sacrificing his life is the only price the ghoul expects as a precondition for taking the lives of his enemies.

The disciple of revenge is a creature who is ready to perish in order to reincarnate as the atrocious nightmare people refer to as vengeance.

2

He dispatched slaves to bring back sorcerers accompanying caravans heading to the north and soothsayers returning from trips to the east, west, or south. He closeted himself for long periods with these men and conversed with them at length before he headed out to the crowd with the lethal amulet that wiped out women, baffled sages, shook husbands, and turned the life of the oasis into a continual funeral. A day did not pass without men carrying on their shoulders a litter of poles on which the corpse of a woman lay. They would take her to a burial site on which they piled the stones of a mausoleum.

Children became motherless orphans, men married to the most captivating brides became widowers, and fathers grieved for beloved daughters. Then the oasis experienced chaos because of the calamity's terror, and people investigated the secret of the epidemic in every nook and cranny, consulting sorcerers, diviners, and novice masters. They intercepted passing caravans to debate with travelers, wayfarers, and merchants who might have encountered a comparable epidemic during their unending travels—or who might have heard one day about a tribe afflicted in a similar fashion. But these people in transit and merchants declared that they knew of no epidemic that discriminated between men and women. In the history of the entire desert, they had never heard of a plague that afflicted beautiful women but spared the camel corps. They were unanimous in saying that the matter doubtless concealed an ignoble secret and that the citizens really ought to launch an investigation into the conspiracy, because an affair that the Spirit World did not establish in the ancient Law must be attributable to human volition.

In the early days, doubts hovered around the hero, and accusations—which directed fingers of blame at him alone—lolled on people's tongues. The demise of his wife, however, quelled that rumor and dispelled suspicions about him.

The cunning strategist rubbed his hands together gloatingly and proceeded to send lethal gifts to his victims. He knew that the enigmatic creature generations have referred to as "woman" could fend off every adversity, conquer every obstacle, and abstain from every treat, but could not refuse a single gift fashioned from this base metal. If not for gold, woman would never have succumbed to men's depravities and would never have become a sacrificial offering in the snares of revenge. At the very time that the oasis's longtime herald—who was a man of such diminutive stature citizens compared him to a rooster—rushed around to warn people against accepting suspicious presents or introducing toxic substances into their dwellings, the disciple of retribution placed between the lips of a counterherald a subliminal message and paid him to scurry about repeating a call that sounded reasonable: "We are only deceived by what we love. We only die of what we desire."

3

Shortly after the scarecrow's master took control of the oasis, he ordered the construction of a governor's mansion on the height beside the temple in the northeastern suburb. The annihilation of women had scarcely commenced when the contractors finished their work. Then this glorious mansion, which was circular and encircled by a wall that was also round, gleamed white on the hilltop like one of those jinni fortresses discussed in the epics of the first peoples. For this reason, rubbernecks, riffraff, and rumormongers dubbed it "The Sorcerer's House" even before construction workers finished the building and coated it with the lime stucco that lent it the mysterious quality that enchanted everyone who saw it.

The leader (or the sorcerer, as rumormongers liked to call him) settled into his new castle at the same time that bedlam peaked and houses were depleted of housewives. The only sound to be heard from dwellings was the wail of orphaned offspring. Men wandered aimlessly in the alleys, plazas, and markets—oblivious to their surroundings—like madmen or idiots. The oasis was on the brink of destruction, and its men sensed a lethal void. They were afflicted by maladies attributable to the absence of women. Many noblemen died as a result of this disaster. Finally people were obliged to voice what they had only been averring secretly. They denounced the leader as a sinister creature whose era had brought the oasis no good. Instead, calamities had swooped down on its head since the first day he was chosen. They reminded each other of the slaughter of nobles, using language that included suspicious allusions and intimations.

The governor, though, like any head of state, was conscious from day one that citizens were secretly cursing him (because these fools did not realize that cursing never escapes the governor's attention even when secret, even when not uttered, even if it is merely a thought in a person's mind). What, then, if this name-calling were a statement launched by a tongue and heard by another creature that was keen to consume it? He had, however, not paid any attention to this, because he was sure that people would inevitably curse someone, and that if they could not find any other target, they would curse their governor. If people feared a governor's tyranny, they would curse the Spirit World that had installed this governor.

The sorcerer's knowledge of people's innate nature led him to ignore what was said—and indeed to disparage everything spouted by commoners—but certainly also caused him to be extremely wary once the agitation increased, the chaos became pronounced, and people dared to curse their head of state in the streets, because this was another sign that could lead to anarchy, insurrection, or some other form of recklessness that could threaten the lives of the people, if the governor did not pay attention and did not counter this danger with an appropriate plan.

In these circumstances, it was necessary for a figure who had agreed to govern people to intervene decisively—not to humor people but to shield them from their own savagery.

4

The leader met with the vassals, who had replaced the Council of Sages as his advisers after the sages had been eliminated. The chief vassal said, "Yesterday, master, the first victims of the emptying of the oasis of women fell dead."

He was reclining on a chaise longue that artisans had crafted from palm planks and upholstered with padded strips of leather. He was gazing at the emptiness of the naked sky, which was still, nonchalant, and generously washed by a flood of twilight rays. He was lost in space for a long time. Then he asked carelessly, without ending his celestial romp, "To which victims does the chief vassal refer?"

"The rivalry of two suitors for a girl who had not yet turned fourteen; one struck his rival a fatal blow with a dagger."

The wily strategist's eyes gleamed with sarcasm, but he did not return from his jaunt in the gilded, blue void. He asked dismissively, "Have men begun to understand what it means for man to lose woman—to live in a settlement without any females?"

"The elders of the oasis agree, master, that the absence of women from the fatherland is an enormous evil, even though they would not deny that their presence may also constitute an even greater evil."

"Do they finally realize that woman is a tribulation, no matter the circumstances?"

"The truth is that the intellectuals aren't embarrassed to state bluntly that the desert will never be a true desert till the day it loses all its women."

He taunted the group sarcastically: "Now oasis citizens find themselves living in the desert while the wasteland tribes live comfortably in the shade of the oasis, because they did not lose their quota of women during their migrations."

Sorrow gleamed in Abanaban's eyes, which were washed by the heavenly spring of tears. "My master is right. We are wretches now. No community in the desert, master, is more wretched!"

The leader turned toward him, although his eyes remained locked on the grim void. "Did the chief vassal lose his wife as well?"

The distress in Abanaban's eyes became even more pronounced. He buried his head in his arms and replied in a murmur like a whisper, "Did my master think my wife could escape a trap that has been the destiny of all the women?"

The sorcerer sat up straight and directed his eyes ever higher until the bodyguards feared their master might fall over backward. He subsided into his prayer, as if searching the stern, eternal void for a sign—as if pursuing prophecy's star that appears only as afternoon ends, as if hunting for an allusion that the crowd of ignoramuses gathered around him had ignored. This symbol had selected him from the crowd the way inspiration chooses advocates of purity. In his wily eye, deep-seated irony evolved into true malice, because anyone who responds to the Spirit World's sign inevitably dandles some enigma in his eye.

He volunteered nonchalantly, "I am dying of curiosity to know what people are plotting. I will give a female camel to anyone who tells me what men, whose bedchambers the Spirit World has robbed of women, are plotting."

He released a muffled, murky laugh that reminded the group of that ignoble, mysterious, ugly laugh they commonly heard from the scarecrow in the fields.

The chief vassal covered his eyes with his veil. Then Asen'fru, the tax collector, responded, "Your men are plotting nothing but despair, master."

"I will never think it credible that a man who discovers he is alone in bed at night, without a woman, can close his eyes before he has plotted some treacherous scheme to reclaim his lost treasure."

Asen'fru replied with despair that channeled the people's despair: "That would be futile, master. I fear that those my master refers to as men have been changed by the calamity into dull-witted wraiths who wander the earth like imbeciles."

The master remained still. He was touring the mansions of the eternal void, which was bathed by a golden flood. He tarried in those blue labyrinths for a long time and then said cryptically, "I don't think that the groups you call imbeciles will be slow to respond if we ask for their assistance in changing the homeland of the neighboring tribes into a wasteland, and in transforming our oasis into a real oasis again."

The men bobbed their turbans nervously, and more than one voice murmured, "I don't understand."

The wily strategist explained with the intonation of a soothsayer reciting a prophecy that the horizon had provided: "Not long ago we agreed that an oasis without women is a desert and that a desert populated by women is a true oasis. Don't we have the right to resort to the sword to wrest our share of women by the blade of the sword—as our ancestors did—to return lost life to our wretched oasis?"

The crowd stared at him with astonishment, but he gazed at the empty void with increased curiosity. His eyes narrowed till the ignoble sign vanished from them. Then he asked rhetorically, "Do you think this group of village idiots will be slow to take up spears or swords if we beat the attack drums and send the herald out to tour the alleys with a call to arms?"

Astonishment registered in the men's eyes. Then the soothsayer completed his prophecy: "The generations have never witnessed a single man who postponed a trip to find a woman. You can rest assured that you will find those you think fools become the most ferocious of men the moment they understand that the point of the raid is capturing women!"

Stillness prevailed.

Outside, the children's weeping and the clamor of people passing in the streets echoed even more loudly.

THE RAIDS

1

"Hee, hee, hee, hee, hee—a hunt wouldn't be called a hunt if woman wasn't the prey. Raids wouldn't really be raids if woman wasn't the booty. Hee, hee, hee."

According to accounts of informed sources, during the attacks that the tribe's mounted warriors launched against both the tribes inhabiting neighboring deserts and the peoples lurking in dark forest recesses, the ruler liked—while directing his enigmatic eyes to the clear sky and covering his nose with his gloomy veil—to unleash repeatedly, like a lunatic, his muffled, detestable laughter, which resembled the chortles of the dreadful scarecrow that had been erected in the open fields (as if he were some demonic rebel jinni).

He also enjoyed climbing to the roof terraces of his glorious edifice to discern in the dust at the horizons the homecoming of hordes of heroes bearing this unique booty that populated the wastelands, transforming them into homelands, whereas their abduction transformed those nations into a desolate wasteland. Then he would share this good news with members of his entourage: "I wager that the horizons are sending us hunters bringing back booty!" He would remind the vassals of the circumstances of the miserable creatures who had grown languid and whose backs had been broken by the disappearance of women till they roamed the streets like idiotic wraiths. The seductive riot he had added to the raid's goal had transformed those men. The paradise that is woman had turned the wimps into totally different creatures. He would growl his dark laugh before sharing a proverb with them: "If you wish to conquer your enemy, discontinue raids for spoils and convince your army that the goal of the campaign is paradise, that the goal of the terror is the abduction of women. Hee, hee, hee. . . ." He would not let the opportunity escape to end his mockery with a little joke: "Once you experience the delight of the chase when the prey is a beautiful woman, you'll be surprised to find that you have all changed into heroes."

He descended that day from his glorious fortress to welcome the campaign's legions of warriors as he always did. He hastened to meet the combatants—but not to greet them, check on their condition, examine them to reassure himself about their good health, or congratulate those who had returned to their homes in one piece; he sped there instead to choose his share of the booty. He approached the Oases Gate or the Gate of the Western Hammada and stationed himself at the portal, surrounded by his retinue. He stopped the warriors' caravans at the entrance and ordered that the goods be unloaded from the pack animals. He had the women promenade in the plaza for a long time while he strutted among them, checking their figures, breasts, legs, faces, and teeth. Yes, yes. . . . He liked to examine their teeth with intense interest. He was said to have remarked in one of his assemblies that a woman is like a horse; her secret is located between her jaws. He finally chose his share of the booty at a rate of one head from each mounted warrior, as per the edict he had decreed for the combatants shortly before the launch of the campaign. The troops had kidded him—some referring to this as a customs tariff and others calling it a toll.

Once the governor made his pick, he ordered the cavalcade to proceed. Then the special forces troops rushed home to stash their beauties in the corners of their homes. Most soldiers were content with one woman—or two in rare circumstances. Like herders corralling goats, they drove the remaining women to the markets of the oasis to display for auction.

2

Successive generations recount that the first booty in the history of the razzia was not herds of cattle (as in the first eras when the most ancient inhabitants domesticated bovines). It was not herds of horses (as in subsequent eras when horses became treasures for the sons of the desert). It was not caravans of camels (as in the later periods when camels entered the wilderness). Instead, the trophy from day one was woman.

It was actually said that wars arose between tribes only because of her and that feuds between clans flared up only to gain control of her or to recapture her from the grip of a rival faction, because the early times witnessed a grievous shortage of the community of women for some unknown reason that baffled the soothsayers and that scholars struggled to explain. Some said this occurred pursuant to a wisdom the Spirit World intended for the tribes' benefit, because a plenitude of women would lead to a plenitude of civil strife. That tendency diminished when there were fewer women, because one woman could satisfy all the men, whether they wished to partner with her for fun or for offspring. Another clique said that the reason for the scarcity of women had something to do with the existence of woman herself, because her existence had led to the original enmity that had induced one brother to raise his hand to kill his brother in order to master her and monopolize her for himself. When the Spirit World saw the appetite of the son of the desert and his thirst for possession and enmity, it deposited a secret in woman's womb, restricting her to bear only male offspring in order to stock the wars with the cannon fodder they needed. Then males were born in abundance, because they would go to die in conflicts, raids, and wars; wombs rarely produced females—for fear of the suffering that this blithe creature would experience should her protectors die in the wars.

People of the desert did agree, however, that all desert dwellers were descended from the womb of a woman who had been abducted. To prove the certainty of this claim, they cited the taboo of desert people against that woman's naming her mate, for whose origins the generations give no history, affirming that their original grandmother harbored rancor against their grandfather, because he had stolen her from her father's home. So, in revenge, she had sworn never to reveal his name. People repeated in their epic poetry that the original grandmother would retreat from time to time to a corner of her dwelling, and succumb to a lengthy bout of weeping. She chided her man for cowardice and told him he would not have been able to retain her for a split second had her father still been alive.

From this ancient dirge the wily strategists of the various tribes derived a proverb. They instructed their mounted warriors: "A woman is like a serpent. You will never be safe from its evil unless you decapitate it, and you behead a woman by beheading the man standing behind her."

The generations learned from experience that a man cannot enjoy a woman if a single male relative of hers remains alive.

3

The oasis relied on its sons' swords and embraced the good life. Well-being returned to its citizens, and the columns of beautiful women—who continued to arrive at the gates of the oasis like so many head of cattle—served as a curative antidote for their uncanny ailments. Fascinating women of every color, community, and race crowded together in the interiors of all the dwellings until the walls could scarcely hold them. Houses overflowed with these incredible female treasures, and caravans set out to search for treasures only as presents for these feminine treasures. Then, as a result of the generosity of these treasures, other treasures spilled into the alleyways, which handed on a share to the streets, which granted a portion to the markets. Then merchants from passing caravans also acquired a share of this flood and traveled with mixed race, black, and white beauties to the four corners of the desert. During that period the oasis experienced a delight it had never known before, because adolescents and young men embraced foreign girls in the plazas, alleys, and streets, and farmers mated with beautiful women alfresco near the scarecrow on their return from the fields. Male poets and vocalists sang all night long outside their homes while music buffs danced. They drummed in a celebratory fashion even on nights when the moon was not visible from the oasis and its streets were inundated by tenebrous darkness.

In that era, oasis citizens learned about houses that shelter women who offer enjoyment to any man who pays her a fee.

Back in that era, too, the hero—Ah'llum—left the oasis, led by one of his slaves. He pronounced a withering jeremiad before slipping through the Gate of the Western Hammada, where the wasteland swallowed him once and for all. It was said back then that the hero had decided to save himself. The original ancestors had been the first to warn against lingering long on an earth where there were many women, because women were like armies of locusts, which inevitably bring disaster when they enter the homes of a people.

Forgetful folks did not know that prophecy in the desert travels only via the tongues of the blind. People from ancient times have learned from experience that only a person who has lost his sight is granted the blessing of insight. For this reason, the sages believed in blind clairvoyants and disavowed sighted claimants to prophecy. For this reason, too, blind diviners were the most renowned in the desert; they did not err in seeing—in their tenebrous darkness—what the Spirit World was planning.

4

The wait for the prophecy did not last long.

The wait for the prophecy was not prolonged, because the Unknown, which administers its affairs in the Spirit World, ignores fools who are beguiled by a fraudulent blessing they mistake for an eternal paradise. The Unknown, which weaves together threads of danger in dark crannies, pays no heed when stupid men rely on enjoyment and devote themselves to lethal fun and games that spawn lassitude. Ignoble lassitude—which spares no one who succumbs to it—makes a fool of, dandles, and seduces its victim till he is reassured by its embraces. Then it draws the sword of danger from its scabbard and plunges the blade in the victim's throat up to the hilt.

Stupid men drowned in luxury and yielded to the embrace that claimed it would grant them lost happiness. Then, like specters disguised as belles, it led them astray only to cast them into the mouth of the dragon. The ignoble specter plucked memory from the minds of the griots, replacing it with forgetfulness. This was evident when they forgot the first commandment, which says that woman resembles a serpent, whose evil threatens you until you decapitate it, and that you behead a woman by beheading the man who stands behind her.

No one knows how that happened.

No one knows how one of these men abducted the daughter of the leader from Azjirr. This dread hero gathered armies from all the tribes and marched them to besiege the miserable oasis in a manner unprecedented in all the desert's long history.

The sorcerer awoke at dawn one day and mounted the roof terrace of his fortress as he normally did each morning. Then by the dawn's dim light, he found encircling the walls from every direction—swarming like locusts—as many soldiers as there are pebbles. The empty countryside was black with them all the way to the farthest horizons.

THE BEAUTY

1

Couriers from the raiding warriors arrived shortly after daybreak with a message for the governor of the oasis. They dismounted and approached the sorcerer to present him with the strangest message. From a linen wrapper, they produced a ravishing doll that represented a beautiful young woman, whose large, kohl-rimmed eyes gleamed with a captivating smile. Her oval cheeks, which were fashioned from an elephant's tusk, were rouged a dark red. Braids of black hair cascaded from her head to fall over a jutting breast as taut as a bowstring. A kerchief the blood red color of a sorrel hibiscus blossom was fastened around her head. Her loose-fitting dress, which was gleaming white, was adorned with talismanic designs embroidered with silk thread. Around her ivory neck hung a massive necklace made of coral imported from countries situated on the seashores of the North.

The dazzled sorcerer examined the doll and murmured in the whisper a person uses to address himself: "This is the most ingenious doll I've ever seen! This is the most marvelous one I've ever encountered!" Then the couriers handed him the second half of the message: a genuine skull—depressing and dark—that dirt and time had ravaged, corroding its bones in places. The uncanny sign in its empty eye sockets would certainly have afflicted with tremors anyone who saw it. This skull was wrapped in a worn snakeskin, which the sorcerer removed. A pronounced pallor crept across his face, and he muttered with alarm he did not succeed in hiding: "What's this?"

But the couriers did not respond to his question with a single word. They left him—as he clutched the doll in his right hand and the skull in the left—and rode away.

2

The leader ordered the oasis's covens of diviners to be brought to him and then placed the message before them. He stood over them, waiting for their interpretation. Although enthusiasts, counterfeiters, and imposters have always welcomed invitations like these (perhaps to flaunt their gifts before the crowd), they differed in their readings of the message's symbolism and did not succeed in deciphering the meaning that the author of the message had concealed in the symbol—despite the enticement of the generous reward the governor had announced for anyone who offered a convincing interpretation.

Feeling desperate, the governor dispatched the herald again.

The herald made the rounds of the streets and passed through the markets of itinerant caravans, shouting out the call while emphasizing his master's promise to reward generously anyone who found in himself a genuine aptitude for deciphering the message from the leader of the foreign coalition.

Shortly before evening fell, a member of a passing caravan approached the palace and announced that in his group there was a cunning tactician whose ability to decipher news of the age was unparalleled in the tribes of the South or the cities of the North. He added that the sly dog had refused to come, because he disdained man's affairs and claimed that his mission was not to decipher people's messages, but to unlock the symbols of the heavens' revelations.

The governor was delighted and sent his soldiers to fetch this foreign adviser. When the guards returned, accompanied by the guest, the setting sun was pouring twilight rays generously on the walls of the glorious fortress.

3

He was a specter as dark as coal—a perfectly formed black man. The oasis had never seen a person with such well-proportioned features; he had a lean build, tall stature, and straight nose. His eyes had a friendly look, although the stillness of his pupils reminded people of the absent look of eternal wanderers and hermits.

The governor placed before him the charming doll and stared at the man's eyes with intense curiosity. Then he stretched out his hand to present the skull to him.

The cunning tactician gazed at the message indifferently. No, no— that look was not genuine indifference; it was another type of look. The sorcerer seemed to have discerned the glance's symbolism, because he acted to forestall the master of the sign from voicing his idea.

The governor said, "Don't tell me that my message is a script from a heavenly message, not a human one. Know that the fate of this nation, which has fed you when you were hungry and kept you safe from fear—just as it has fed and offered security to many before you—is concealed in the damn riddle you hold in your hands. So beware!"

An enigmatic smile glinted in the eyes of the wily foreigner. No—it was not a genuine smile; it was the shadow of a smile, a sign preparing the way for the birth of a smile.

Then. . . .

Then he spoke. The retinue heard a soft, melodious voice—like the song of the wind blowing in the retem groves. "I'm sad to hear you had trouble deciphering this message."

"What are you saying?"

"Via the doll, the message's author demands back from my master the woman (or women)."

The leader gazed at the man's eyes, which were as beautiful as a gazelle's, and asked attentively, "The leader of the foreigners demands back the woman or the women?"

"The beauty! The leader beyond the gates demands the beauty by means of the doll, master. The perfectly crafted doll in our spoken language means 'beautiful woman,' either in the singular or the plural."

"Beware!"

"A genuine message, like a prophecy, always brooks more than one interpretation."

"We could return the beautiful women from Azjirr's tribes, but how could we return all the women? Can we find for the leader of the foreign coalition his captivating daughter, who was allegedly kidnapped and brought by a warrior through the gates of the oasis one day?"

"I beg forgiveness, but human issues are beyond my purview."

"What about the second half?"

"The second half spells destruction!"

"Destruction?"

"Even children back home know that a skull is a symbol of destruction."

"What destruction are you talking about, wretched alien?"

"If my master will allow, I will read him the message's two parts together."

"Quickly!"

"If the beauty is not returned, your fate will be destruction!"

"What are you saying?"

"This is the message, which was composed in the language of semiosis."

"But, but, this is an ugly threat and not an appropriate communication for one leader to send to another."

"A messenger can do no more than communicate the message."

"This . . . this is an insult, not a message."

"A messenger can do no more than communicate the message."

4

He issued a stern order to the vassals, soldiers, and guards to search for the daughter of the leader of the foreign coalition. So they vied to investigate, searching every room, nook, and cranny in all the houses, but found no trace of the beauty. They scoured the entire oasis and plowed up the fields. Then they returned to stand before their leader. Some trembled with fright and others bowed their heads dejectedly.

The chief vassal stepped forward and stammered, "It seems most likely, master, that she was sold in the markets and that men from some passing caravan bought her."

The leader, whose cheeks were yielding to pallor, stared at him with expressionless eyes. After a period of silence, he asked, "Do you mean that this calamity has departed from the walls of our oasis?"

When the chief vassal nodded in the affirmative, the leader added, "If this female jinni has fled from the oasis, a curse has descended on it."

A new expression passed through the master's eyes—one that was unfamiliar to the soldiers, vassals, and courtiers. It was an expression that no beast in a herd would see in the herder's eyes. It first afflicts those suffering from some unknown angst and eventually casts them into ague's kiln. The onlookers were a miserable community who viewed rulers and powerful figures in the world as gods soaring above the hateful paralysis called "weakness" in the language of the masses.

The way the downtrodden see things, the weakness of sovereigns is always an ill omen.

To fend off the specter of weakness, the chief vassal said, "I would have thought that the arrival of the beauty was the curse, not her flight."

"Would she have run away had she not first settled here? Her flight is a cunning scheme associated with settling here."

"I knew Ah'llum was a hero but have realized only today that he was a diviner too."

". . . ."

"The day he left the oasis he said that when women are plentiful on a patch of earth, a calamity will soon strike there."

"The secret lies in his blindness. The secret lies in the affliction. Blindness turns a creature into a clairvoyant. The affliction makes a man a sage."

"I wonder where he is now."

The leader gazed at him inquisitively. Raising his eyes to the heavens as if to read a prophecy in the grim void, he remarked, "Somewhere in the badlands he is rubbing his hands together with all the intoxication of those who have waited patiently to see the day their revenge is accomplished."

"Revenge?"

"People like him endure the pains of life merely to take revenge. Revenge for them isn't merely a consolation; it is life itself."

"Does my master—like many others—suspect that our friend played a part in decimating the women of the oasis with secret potions?"

The sorcerer journeyed far into the sky's void. There was an uncanny glint in his eyes when he remarked casually, "We shouldn't dwell on what is obvious while ignoring what is covert—either in our judgments or our lives. When the Spirit World frowns in our face, what difference will the means make?"

"Had the women not been decimated, master, we wouldn't have sallied forth to hunt for them. Had the women in our homes not been slain, we would not stand today encircled by massive armies we are powerless to combat."

"When a wanderer is struck by a destiny like this, he must read the message as it ought to be read."

"The message?"

"The Spirit World never wrongs us. If a transitory calamity strikes us, we should welcome the lesson, because it is merely a trial. If the time is ripe for a disaster in our settlements, we can still control it, because we can fashion an ending that terminates the pain."

"If I understand my master's words properly, their import is no doubt painful."

"The Spirit World has placed in our hands the panacea for all pains!"

5

The governor ordered the people's nobles to gather.

He received them on luxurious carpets in the courtyard of his glorious bastion and addressed them tersely: "The leader of the foreign coalition suffocates us with armies we cannot possibly repulse and demands the return of a girl we cannot find. What do you advise?"

The miserable silence that followed reigned for a long time. The leader, who stood facing the group, clasped his hands behind his back and paced east and west, bent forward, as if searching for some bonanza or treasure on the ground. He was starting to speak again when a voice, which erupted from the crowd of noblemen, stopped him. "Did our master ask our opinion on the day he decreed civil strife and raided tribes near and far to snatch women? Did our master assume that a man could lie contentedly in the arms of a woman he had abducted with a sword's blade? Doesn't our master realize that a man who kidnaps a woman by force of arms is a murderer, even if destiny is slow to catch up with him and allows him to live a hundred years?"

A soldier rushed to silence the man forcibly, but the leader gestured sternly for him to desist. When he took two steps toward the assembly, he spotted in the midst of the tribe's elders a thin, scrawny, mature man who was turbaned with a faded veil and who clutched a burnished cane in his trembling hand.

He did not wait for the leader's response. Instead he added in the same daring voice, "We all know, master, that woman is a creature devoid of utility. She not only lacks utility but is actually injurious. Although we know this, we cannot keep ourselves from vying to acquire her. So we value her more than whatever is most precious in the desert and even consider her the crown of all the desert's treasures. Therefore, intellectuals know that kidnapping women by force is a reckless adventure and an enormous danger. The total idiot who commits this offense wouldn't have dared to embark on this madness had he realized that he was condemning himself to destruction. When he is not destroyed by the hand of her husband—if he survives—he is done in by the hand of comrades who pledge their fealty to him although their real goal is his treasure: the woman. When he is not destroyed by the malevolent conspiracies of these men, he is done in by the hand of the woman herself. This mysterious creature, whose secret no man has grasped, will surely poison his food one day, because a woman never forgives a man who abducts her from her father's house—not even if she was abducted with her father's consent. She will continue to harbor rancor and will scout for opportunities for revenge to the final day of her life. The man will never escape her rancor, no matter how many children he fathers for her. He won't escape from her ill will, not even if he grants her ten children from his loins."

This mature man fell silent, and the courtyard was still. The vassals and guards discerned in their lord's eyes a dread shadow, a sign that frightened everyone and afflicted their souls with despair. It was weakness!

The leader unclasped his hands only to clasp them behind his back again. He was going to speak, but one of the notables rushed forward to address the strategist derisively: "I wager that the cunning foreign strategist entrusted that jinni woman to our master's custody precisely because he knew our master is of jinni heritage!"

A noisy muttering spread through the assembled crowd, and the vassals glanced back and forth between the two adversaries with confusion and astonishment.

The sorcerer smiled with the forbearance of the ancient sages. So his interlocutor found the courage to add, "It is said that only a sorcerer can decipher a sorcerer's talisman. The day the Spirit World brought you forth from the innards of your eerie scarecrow, we didn't imagine that you would incite the rabble against us, ruin us with your taxes, or shed the blood of the elite while allowing the proletariat to conquer the earth. Today, when the specter of punishment looms on the horizon, you send lackeys to summon us to the consultative assembly you dissolved."

People anticipated an angry response. People awaited a dreadful response. People expected a veritable earthquake of a response but were surprised to see the leader's head contract that day and shrink toward the leader's chest till it almost vanished in the folds of his dark robe.

His head became an insignificant blister on his shoulders. Then his body immediately began to shake with an alarming tremor. This feverish shaking was accompanied by the sound of muffled laughter—an ignoble, uncanny, detestable rattle that so provoked and poisoned their bodies with shudders and nausea that many people present were sure they confronted at that hour the scarecrow of the fields, and were no longer in the presence of the leader.

The sorcerer, however, caught his breath and popped out of his flask to address the people in clear language. "Woe to anyone who waits for people's gratitude! Woe to a ruler who expects any acknowledgment for a benefaction, because people construe good deeds as evil ones!"

In a far corner, near the exterior wall, a local notable whispered, "For a citizen to dare to address a ruler insolently—our ancestors have warned us—is a harbinger of evil!"

The leader, however, did not notice this whispered comment. Perhaps he did but ignored it. He clasped his hands behind his back and paced in the courtyard for a time. He stopped. Then he said, as if addressing himself, "What you all consider to have been the slaughter of the elite, others consider deliverance from an oppressive group. What some of you think was incitement of the proletariat against the bourgeoisie, others think of as a return of usurped rights to those whose rights they had once been. Today most of you consider the importation of women to have been a foolhardy adventure and evil, but yesterday the majority of you considered it a necessity that saved the lineage from the ghoul of extinction. So what do the people actually want? Or, is there no way to satisfy man, who has a natural tendency toward wild fluctuations, anarchy, and insurrection?"

He advanced two steps toward the assembled crowd and glared at them defiantly and challengingly. Then he tossed out an importunate challenge: "I will give you everything I possess if you answer my question: What does man want?"

You could have heard a pin drop in the courtyard.

THE IDOL

1

During the first stage of the siege, the strategist pinned his hopes on the desert and told the vassals that the wilderness had always been a resource for both landowners with water and enemies raiding other tribes. Rubbing his hands together repeatedly, he had said gloatingly, "The party that lays siege to another group, according to the customary law of the desert, stands outside the walls, far from the water—unlike the group inside the walls where the well of water is located."

But, in only a matter of days, this claim was rebutted, because the belligerent armies—which had supplied their water needs from the well called Harakat at the fringes of the Western Hammada—disrupted the flow of caravans and the importation of food stuffs, which the leader discovered were no less critical than water, because the harvest of the oasis had not been adequate even for the original inhabitants. How could it suffice once the number of inhabitants had multiplied many times, when foreign communities and lineages had crowded into the oasis from distant lands, and when women's wombs—after the recent raids—had supplied it with columns of a new generation (which was, if possible, even more ravenous)?

Realizing that he had miscalculated, the sorcerer reconsidered. He decided to resort to every sorcerer's favorite weapon: an underhanded scheme!

He selected a bevy of the most beautiful women in the oasis and sent them as a gift to the leader of the foreigners. Along with this present he sent an oral message via a spokesman.

In this message, he acknowledged that he had read the leader's message. He lauded its author for his sagacity in crafting its symbolism and said he understood that it was incumbent on him, as a condition for peace, to return the women whom men of his tribes had abducted. So here he was sending the leader a first group of women as a confidence-building gesture. With reference to the rumor that the distinguished leader was demanding the return of his youngest daughter (who was reportedly abducted one day and brought to the oasis), he could assure him truthfully that this claim was false, because he had searched the oasis house by house, nook by nook, and rock by rock, but not discovered the alleged victim. Should any doubt remain in the heart of His Honor the Leader concerning the veracity of this claim, he could send messengers to investigate and to search all the houses and nooks.

The courier returned bearing a new message. This was an identical, equally superb doll, and no detail had been overlooked in its fabrication. The beauty was composed of ivory, linen, goat hair, and silk thread.

The leader called in the caravan's diviner, who had been stranded in the oasis by the siege. He gazed indifferently at the doll and translated the message derisively: "We are still waiting for the beauty!"

"Is that all?"

"I discern no change in its production to distinguish this toy from the first."

"Is there no reference in this message to the offer for an international team of inspectors?"

The soothsayer shook his head no. Then the leader recoiled into his corner like a hedgehog. His head slipped down between his shoulders, but he did not sway with the rattling giggle of the scarecrow of the fields.

2

"Master, I saw an effigy, not a leader. I saw a dreadful effigy, larger than any statue I have ever seen."

The leader sat with his courier, who had returned from the raiders' camps, and listened with intense curiosity to this debriefing. He remained silent and seemed absentminded. Then, still aloof, he inquired, "You mentioned a dreadful effigy?"

"The fact is this wasn't just any oversized doll. It was . . . it was a scarecrow!"

"A scarecrow?"

"A scarecrow just like the scarecrow in our oasis—except the foreigners' was bigger."

"What are you saying?"

"The very sight of it shook me to my core and made me feel dizzy. I had to search for my tongue a long time before I could deliver my master's message to that idol."

"Did the idol speak? Did you hear a voice from the foreigners' idol?"

The messenger wiped away the sweat flowing down his cheeks with the edge of his veil. He sighed deeply before replying, "No."

The leader roamed far away and migrated to his naked, indifferent heavens, which were washed with a radiant blue. When he returned from his travels, he found that his messenger was singing the praises of the lost girl's beauty and reporting that the leader he had seen crammed inside the skins of the hideous scarecrow would never renounce her, because she was as beautiful as the desert moon and men of the tribes could not milk their camels properly on dark nights, when the moon was not visible, unless the tribe's beauty showed her face to them.

3

Once evening fell and the full moon appeared, he stretched out on the courtyard's carpets and requested the female vocalist. He wished to listen to songs as he had often done during the days of lost peace.

The bard plucked the string twice. Then the bird of longing fluttered inside him, and the desert disappeared from the desert. Times were transposed to violate the law of temporal progression by pausing in space. Tears glittered in the sky's eye and winked back and forth between the stars.

Then he sang. . . .

He sang along with the female vocalist in a plaintive voice. Obscure worries enervated him, and his eyes overflowed with a hot liquid like flaming water.

He released a loud cry, wailing as he rotated from right to left. He was trembling violently. Then he collapsed, leaning his back against the wall, and gestured that the party was over.

The singer left, and the chief vassal appeared. He took a seat nearby and gazed anxiously at the master. He searched the legacy of his ancestors for a key to start a conversation. "We have inherited from our pious ancestors their fear of listening to tunes, because music feeds the soul's pain and afflicts bodies with chronic depression."

The ecstatic leader's breathing calmed a little, but he writhed along the wall while he kept his eyes trained on the moon. He mumbled, "What does a person do when he has a thirst he can never quench?"

"A thirst that water cannot quench is satisfied by a beautiful woman, master."

"There is one thirst that not even a beauty can satisfy."

"I bet this thirst is nothing more nor less than yearning."

"Can anything but melodies satisfy a man's yearning?"

"I fear that melodies will prove a short-lived remedy."

"What treatment is there for patients suffering from yearning if melodies provide no cure?"

The chief vassal fell silent and directed his gaze toward a sky that was washed by the moon's deluge. He watched a shooting star that fell to the east and another that fell to the west. In the voice of a person wandering away, he said, "Travels, travels. The only antidote for the pains caused by the Spirit World is travel. The only balsam that treats yearning is travel."

The leader swayed as if dancing. He soon joined the visionary vassal in the distant land: "Travels, travels. Don't you suspect that this word is itself a tune? Don't you know that this word conceals the most exquisite melody? Don't you know that lyrics would not be lyrics if they didn't discuss travels?"

"How could I not know, master, when I was the first devotee of this god? But for him, people of the desert would never have deserved the title of 'desert people.'"

"Do you know I was once a wayfarer too? I was a man the tribes called the sorcerer—the way they do all wayfarers who keep their secrets to themselves. I disliked arriving in a land if I couldn't leave it the next day. I came to the oasis as a wayfarer too, but the walls caught me by surprise the day I decided to use some of my secrets to purchase supplies. I had forgotten that provisions are an ignoble stratagem that evokes whispered temptations in wayfarers who then hunker down on the earth, which enslaves them. The earth's turn ends only when the beauty's turn commences. The day the beauty entered the earth of the fields, I became her captive. I have never left the earth of the fields since."

"The fields?"

"I have been a hostage of the scarecrow since that day."

"The scarecrow?"

"The scarecrow is our destiny. We settle in it. It settles in us. We are the scarecrow, and the scarecrow is us."

"My master was discussing travels."

"The scarecrow is the enemy of travels."

"Frankly, master, I don't understand."

"Trips. Travels. If I didn't long to travel, the siege wouldn't upset me—not even if it lasted a thousand years."

"This is further evidence of the cunning of the foreigners' giant mascot. He knew our secret and grabbed us where it hurt."

"You're right. This ignoble chap knows that a siege for a wayfarer is a harsher punishment than any other."

He fell silent and watched the stars' sign. His eyes gleamed by the light of the full moon. He added cryptically, "If the idol weren't a scarecrow, he wouldn't have been granted much of the Spirit World's knowledge!"

He repeated this prophecy twice.

4

The suffering of the oasis began despite crisis management.

During the first days of the siege, the leader had released a stern command to purchase grain and produce from the caravan markets at market prices, which began to rise once the scent of danger was in the air—as normally happens in chaotic times to any commodity. He encouraged the vassals to offer farmers tempting prices for their crops and continued to press them to spend money lavishly on food supplies, even if that meant expending the last gold coin collected for taxes.

Despite his crisis management, the oasis began to suffer a food shortage after only a few months. Then misgivings tormented people, and sages felt anxious about the fate of their offspring, because they saw the specter of famine hovering over the oasis—which had enjoyed prosperity, affluence, and the good life for years.

Many people grasped the oasis's secret that day. They grasped the secret of that timid child who fears anarchy and therefore flees to the farthest land or is afflicted by paralysis. He is called, in common parlance, "commerce." They realized that the oasis's secret was borrowed from commerce's secret and that the aggressors' scarecrow had been granted much of the science of the Spirit World, because he had terrified the creature that cannot tolerate wars. Then the artery that had supplied New Waw with life throughout these years was severed. The ignoble creature's goal was to starve the masses to death and to prevent the minority that hunger would not kill (because such people were sustained by poetry and plaintive songs) from stepping forth and wandering through the world.

Spellbound folks, who liked to detect a sign in every matter, discovered that the secret the caravans bore, the secret that crossed desert wilderness on beasts of burden, did not merely fashion the splendor of oases but actually created the oases. It built their walls. It brought sons there from parts unknown to reside in the houses, populate the markets, stroll down the streets, and plant crops in its earth. With its own magic hands, it built a civilization from nothing and settled it in the labyrinths of the void as a complex to which a traveler headed—even while suspecting this was another ploy of the mirage.

The painful aspect of the matter, however, is that the secret is a transitory treasure that has no spot to call home save the backs of beasts of burden, and these creatures—like people, like poets—suffer from wanderlust and keep on the move. If a caravan unpacked its secret in a place one day, it would doubtless carry it off on the animals' backs to another location on the morrow.

The afflicted people, who never stopped investigating by interpreting and deciphering news of the times, saw in the flight of the caravans an evil omen presaging the flight of the oasis from its walls.

5

No one knows what the leader was thinking the day he sent the foreign coalition's leader a new bevy: a long column of women. They marched out of the oasis—escorted by couriers instead of the soldiers who had been their escorts the day they first entered the oasis. The aliens' scarecrow's response came in the form of a new talisman: a gray serpent puppet made of camel hair, leather thongs, pieces of fabric, and sticks of wood. This hateful serpent had bloody eyes and a savage snout. It held between its jaws the puppet of a woman with worried eyes and ashen cheeks. She was wrapped in faded rags.

The governor placed the repulsive talisman before the itinerant diviner, who dispassionately translated it into words: "The trick has reclaimed what the treacherous hand took from us."

The message astonished the courtiers, but the sorcerer smiled enigmatically that day. The vassals did not discern in his eyes the ugly expression that always shook them: weakness.

No one grasped that smile's secret meaning till tongues repeated news of the spread of an epidemic in the enemy ranks and the destruction of dreadful numbers of soldiers. Then gossips spread the rumor that this epidemic was transmitted to the enemy camp through the women's clothes. Commenting on the outbreak, the leader said in the courtyard of his glorious fortress: "Woman, who brought bad luck into the oasis's dwellings yesterday, can transport it to the enemy's dwellings today."

The sorcerer's delight with the epidemic did not, however, last long, because one morning, when he climbed to the fort's roof terraces and studied the nearby wasteland where the raiders' forces were stationed, he saw a black mass covering the wilderness and stretching to the horizon in every direction. He observed as many creatures as there are pebbles. They were clinging to the hospitable wasteland like ticks to the hide of a camel. New convoys of soldiers—spawned continually by the Unknown—cloaked the earth till not an inch of it was visible. They advanced quickly and made the corners of the earth shake till the ground itself seemed to be quaking and moving—rather than the creatures streaming across it.

The sight terrified him, and a paralyzing impotence flowed through his body. He was absent for a long time but finally grumbled to himself: "No. These aren't Azjirr's tribes. No, since day one we haven't been fighting against wasteland tribes. The tribes are from the Spirit World! That hideous idol was never the leader of Azjirr. Every sign points to the fact that the creature was of jinni descent. How could I have missed this? Why didn't I see this before?"

THE SACRIFICIAL OFFERING

1

He disguised himself in the tattered garments of shepherds, slipped out the servants' gate, and gazed at the sky, which was decorated with garlands of stars. His eyes sparkled with an enigmatic glint. He listened carefully but heard only the stillness. He descended from the heights and crossed the temple plaza. He turned north and entered the alleys. The walls' shadows swallowed him for a long way. Before he emerged from the last alleyway, he remembered the council and pondered how base specters called prominent citizens had sullied his actions and turned his good deed into an evil one. They had not been satisfied with distorting or corrupting it; they had gone even farther, spoken maliciously, and secretly conspired to commit evil. They had not merely revealed their loathsome faces; their vengeful eyes had glared at him with an ill-omened gleam when he extracted powerful despair from his body the way tweezers draw a thorn from the foot. Then weakness flooded his soul. Could he forgive them this vengeful signal at the only hour when governors need sympathy that they do not expect from strangers, because they normally are the ones extending sympathy to strangers?

He traversed the lanes, which were masked by rows of walls, and took the route leading to the fields. The singing of the grasshoppers grew louder, and the smell of grass and moist earth assailed his nostrils. This was water's smell. This was water's perfume. This was water's secret—water's smell that dolts do not detect, not realizing that water moves all the things that scents pervade. Water crosses dead earth and imbues its dirt with a smell. It descends deep into the earth to reach seeds buried in mattamore pits. It revives them and infuses them with its breath to grant them an odor. Even when it tires of playing underground and decides to leave the earth and return to its homeland by evaporating—rising in vapors, passing through the air—it leaves a scent in the void. Water! It has no odor but lavishly grants odors. It has no color but lavishly grants colors. It has no taste but lavishly grants all tastes. Is this not sufficient proof that this entity belongs to the Spirit World?

He crossed the brook. The mysterious liquid gleamed in the irrigation ditches by the light of the stars. The smell of grass, mud, and fig trees grew more intense. He slipped off his sandals and placed them under his arm. He lowered his right foot into the water and sank his left foot into the brook's mire. He waded in the mud for a stretch and then retraced his steps. The song of the grasshoppers rose like melancholy hymns. He slowly removed his baggy shorts and pulled off his tunic as well. He loosened his head wrap and began to free himself of his veil. He bundled his clothes together and threw them far away. He knelt on the earth and plunged into the mire. The noble liquid flooded over him, teased his limbs, tickled his armpits, and caressed his entire body. Then he sighed ecstatically and sniffed the humid air, which water perfumed with its unknown scent.

He began the process of rehydration as water flowed through his body and he flowed through the mire's body. He did not sink into the mud; instead the mud sank into him. The pores of his body opened to allow mud to enter, and mud's pores opened to allow him to penetrate them with all his suppleness, virility, and fluidity. Then he yielded and disappeared in order to struggle with a thirst that swallowing water does not quench. It is a thirst that can be tamed only when a thirsty person renounces his pride and becomes part of the water, the mud, the marriage of dirt and water, earth and sky, wasteland and Spirit World. He wallowed. He crawled right, turned north, and moaned ecstatically. Then he relaxed every muscle of his body and stretched out.

In the earth's thickets the hymn of the grasshoppers resounded. In the sky's expanses stars spoke.

He crawled toward the veil.

He reached the leather figure positioned near the north brook. He crawled up this specter's frame and glided into its coarse fabric the way a snake glides into its den. He entered the veil to replace the veil. He fled from the scarecrow to take refuge in the scarecrow. He fled from the real scarecrow to shelter in the leather scarecrow erected in the fields. He liberated himself from a scarecrow that inhabited him—a scarecrow hostile to him—to settle as a guest in the belly of another scarecrow.

He freed himself the way a snake does when it sloughs off its skin. He did not merely liberate himself; he was reborn in a new body.

From this body, which was enveloped in the gloom, a mysterious hiss rattled.

2

The chief vassal said, "Famished people are grumbling, master."

They were strolling in the courtyard of the glorious fortress. The sun was kneeling to the west, and the eastern wall was bathed by twilight's rays. The vanquished forces of the mirage, however, resisted desperately before they shot off into seclusion—leaving behind robust trails—and then climbed the neighboring walls.

The leader clasped his hands behind his back before asking, "Is a sovereign even sovereign over a public catastrophe? What strategy can a commander adopt against a problem that he had no role in creating?"

Anxiety settled into Abanaban's eyes. His trembling hand reached out to adjust his veil around his cheeks. Straightening a veil is always a subterfuge to conceal nervousness or mask emotion. After a long silence he ventured, "I don't feel able to offer any advice today; but, master, I do wish to save anything I can. This is what drives me to bare my heart to my master and to discuss the custom that obliges a ruler to feed his subjects."

"I know. I know the Law holds a ruler responsible for the welfare of his subjects. I know, too, that we can't buy their obedience with anything but food. I know, finally, that the sovereign loses his title to sovereignty if he fails to provide these two things: security and bread!"

Upset, he paused and stared at a corner of the wall. He continued with a different refrain: "But don't forget that this is the Law of Peace— not the Law of War. Wartime dictates a different Law. Otherwise war wouldn't be called war, and nations wouldn't tremble in fright at the mere mention of the word."

"I haven't cast doubt on my master's wisdom nor have I questioned his knowledge of the Law of Governors. I simply wanted to draw my master's attention to the danger of civil unrest, because spies have reported that the stink of anarchy is in the air!"

"Everyone knows that prosperity in the oasis depends on it welcoming merchant caravans. Everyone knows as well that the war has frightened away the caravans, which have changed their routes, depriving us of both their goods and the taxes on these goods. So where can I obtain food for the hungry?"

Twilight's rays, which had been bathing the eastern ramparts, retired, and the mirage's tongues, which had been climbing those walls, scattered. The chief vassal said in a disturbing tone, "The day before yesterday they harvested the last edible palm core from the top of the last surviving palm tree in the fields!"

"The last palm?"

"And yesterday a patrol found a pile of human bones buried in a pit near the eastern wall."

"What do you mean?"

Abanaban was silent for a time. When he replied, his voice sounded even stranger: "I'm trying to say that a man who preys on his brother's flesh is not to be trusted."

The leader appeared deflated but did not turn toward his companion. Instead, he continued to stare at a patch of dirt veiled by the evening's shadows. As if finding himself among people for the first time, he observed, "I wouldn't have thought man would ever be capable of doing that."

"Hunger, master, ravishes the mind, and once the mind is lost, so is the man."

"In the desert, people bury themselves in their tents during famines and don't leave them till they're dead."

"The desert has different laws."

"In the desert, they combat hunger by hunting wild animals. Then if a man is lucky and returns with game, he sends half to the leader and divides the rest with his entire hamlet!"

"Different laws apply in the desert, master.

"In the oasis they grumble and challenge authority, wanting to grab bread from the leader's hand."

"This is the law of the oasis, master."

"If they were a community that acknowledged a good deed, that would be easy—or have you forgotten how the nobles disavowed me the day the council met?"

"No good deed goes unpunished, master—that's human nature."

"From day one, I helped the downtrodden among them. I removed the tax burden from the shoulders of poor people, craftsmen, and farmers. I allowed their merchants to trade with gold. So life was revived, our standard of living was good, and everyone was happy."

"Denial of a favor is a human characteristic, master."

"During a calamity, all I see in their eyes is a thirst for vengeance. What right have I to pardon these wretches' mistreatment of me and give them bread, thus decreasing my own nourishment?"

"They claim our master foresaw this crisis, purchased all the wheat in the markets of the oasis, and then buried it secretly underground, the way sorcerers do."

"I will give them all my stockpiles of wheat if you promise that this gift will buy me their fealty for a single day."

"I won't ever do that, master, because I know that man will never pardon a good deed."

"Never pardon a good deed?"

"Yes, master. Man can forgive a bad deed but never a good one!"

He paused and turned his whole body to face his companion. Gazing into his master's eyes with astonishment, the chief vassal saw he was trembling.

He stammered, "What a harsh prophecy!"

His eyes glinted with a haughty flash, and he added with profound submission, "A harsh prophecy is the noblest kind."

3

This prophecy confirmed his hunch and inspired his journey to the veil.

This prophecy completed the inspiration that had caused him to despair during the first days of the disaster.

This prophecy finished fashioning the indistinct whisper, adding form and substance to it.

Now he could continue with his project.

Now he could shed his doubts and approach the Spirit World by realizing his intentions.

Only now did he know for certain that people who consider a good deed an unforgivable offense deserve no mercy. He had hesitated for a long time before offering the monumental sacrifice that the Spirit World had imposed on him as a condition for saving him from every mighty trap, but this noble conduct had not raised him to the ranks of the virtuous. Instead, he had dropped to the level of fools.

Now, after achieving this certainty, he could discard his scruples and venge himself on a community that had repaid his ancient benefaction with nothing but a ruse. He would take revenge, because he himself—like any human being—had never been anything more than the sacrificial victim of an act of vengeance. Yes, from the very beginning man has always been a miserable sacrificial victim offered to compensate for some previous vengeful act; he has therefore been forced to seek revenge as well. He must take his revenge quickly if he wishes to avoid becoming the victim of another vengeful deed and being forced again out of a lair by stings.

4

"Anyone who offers me his allegiance, come hell or high water, receives my guarantee that he will not feel hunger again or suffer from fear."

The herald set off early in the morning with this announcement, and people flocked into the streets. Residents raced through the alleys—men and women, graybeards and youngsters—to climb the hill. Then they besieged the glorious fortress just as foreign tribes were besieging the walls of the oasis.

The soldiers forced them to halt in the audience chamber and form queues. The master made an appearance and repeated his talisman: "Anyone who offers me his allegiance, come hell or high water, receives my guarantee that he will not feel hunger again or suffer from fear."

They roared their approval and wept before him from delight. Then they advanced in columns toward the soldiers to accept their ration of wheat.

In that crowd, from somewhere in the rear, a loud, stern voice rang out, sounding as if the speaker had never known the taste of hunger and had never been importuned by his children's complaints at home. "The food's poisoned! Watch out!"

No one heeded his warning. People kept moving forward in their lines, dragging their feet like exhausted captives who had crossed the desert on foot. They bowed to the soldiers and then received their portion of a gift that would deliver them from hunger and safeguard them from fear.

The soldiers, for their part, did not heed the warning either; perhaps they did not care.

The voice cried out again: "This is a banquet, and a banquet is always a trap. So beware!"

The cry was lost in the din once more. Then the creature hidden in the crowd screamed out a new prophecy: "Once he captured your best men with gifts at a banquet; now he captures you as well—with party favors!"

No one heeded his cry. No one paid any attention to his existence, because hunger's sovereignty has always proved stronger than prophecy's.

5

The soldiers finished transporting the dead palm trunks from the fields and then piled giant pyres of logs and planks in the temple plaza to create a bonfire bigger than any ever seen in the desert before.

The leader ordered the citizens to gather inside the ring of firewood and then positioned himself on the hill by the gate of the glorious fortress. He waited until everyone was silent and then spoke with the harsh terseness he had learned from the language of prophecies. "When I promised one day that if you pledged allegiance to me, come hell or high water, I would deliver you from hunger and fear, I took a solemn oath. Then I fed you and fulfilled half my oath. Now the time has come for me to fulfill the second half."

He gestured to the chief vassal, and Abanaban raised his hand as a signal to the soldiers, who immediately rushed to set fire to the wood.

Screams resounded, and voices cried for help.

People shoved each other aside, trying to escape from the circle of fire, desperate to save themselves, but the soldiers stabbed them with swords and spears. Many fell to the ground, bleeding profusely, and then were trampled underfoot by the mob. Others retreated only to be choked by waves of smoke. They perished, like the rest, in the tongues of flame.

Despite the ferocity with which the soldiers guarded the ring around the fearsome hearth, the will to survive—the will to live—proved stronger than all the ploys of these clever technicians, and fugitives escaped here and there. Then they raced across the naked earth on their way to the Western Hammada Gate, but specters rushed at them there, too, and felled them with arrows and lances.

This holocaust lasted a long time.

The soldiers polished off the civilians, and that night the leader hosted a banquet for his troops to repay them for the expert execution of their duties. They were not, however, destined to enjoy another sunrise, because the poison that their master had mixed into the food proved fast-acting, and they perished in no time at all.

6

The next morning the leader climbed to the roof terraces of the glorious fortress accompanied by the chief vassal. He contemplated the soldiers' corpses, which were strewn around the hill, and gazed at the fearsome hearth—cluttered with ashes, charred wood, and pieces of bone—from which plumes of smoke rose. He looked up at the clear, arrogant, indifferent sky, and tears filled his eyes as he said, "This is the sacrificial offering!"

The chief vassal beside him swayed and wailed in a voice that was not his own: "How harsh is the vengeance of lords! How cruel is the vengeance of lords!"

The master repeated in a voice that also was not his own, "This is the sacrificial offering!"

Stillness was pervasive, a stillness that seemed appropriate for an oasis where only the dead remained. The stillness lasted for some time.

Then the master asked, "Should we lament the destruction of a creature who forgives a bad deed but never a good one?"

The chief vassal lamented, "Man doesn't forgive a good deed, master, because he is a man; man doesn't forgive a good deed, because he rejects shackles and doesn't want to be encumbered by obligations to others."

"Even though such madness doesn't give this creature any right to expect mercy, I fulfilled my promise—as you have seen. I saved them from fear after I fed them to deliver them from hunger. No enemy will ever harm them, and no evil will ever befall them."

"Even if a creature fears pain, he would rather slither across the ground with no limbs—provided he remains alive—than swallow a panacea that spares him pain's evil but costs him his life."

"This is another argument that confirms that this arrogant creature does not rise much above the level of vermin."

"All the same, the desert loses its splendor and becomes a desolate wasteland once man leaves its realm. Look at the oasis, master! Don't you see that this is no longer an oasis? Don't you see that what was an oasis yesterday has become an empty space we could call anything but an oasis?"

The leader did not reply, and a stillness befitting a place populated only by the dead settled over it.

This stillness did not last long.

A blade emerged from a sleeve, the light of the morning sun washed over it, and then it descended like lightning to pierce a chest. The chief vassal staggered and stumbled back. He emitted a subdued groan before mastering himself and taking a few steps forward till he was beside his master, who whispered sadly, "Forgive me. A man who chooses to flee from his enemies must avoid leaving any witnesses behind."

The wounded man grasped the dagger's handle and, with the forbearance of the ancients, replied, "I knew my master would inevitably do this one day."

"I've been forced to join the ranks of the caravan you said could pardon a bad deed but not a good one. You've done me many favors, and now you're receiving your just reward!"

"My master can rest assured that I shall bear no grudge against him, because what he has done proves that my master belongs to the human race."

His pains silenced him, but he struggled stubbornly to withstand the blow and tried to pull the dagger from his chest. He staggered a step forward and then two steps back. He moaned grievously before falling to his knees and then collapsing on the roof terrace.

Rays of morning light illuminated his eyes, in which the master saw all the profundity, peacefulness, and symbolism of a smile.

7

He vanished into the chambers of the fortress and disguised himself in a shepherd's tattered garments. He descended the northeast side of the hill and cast a searching look at the heavens. The luminous disc was settled at the heart of the sky, and all beings swam in the mirage's tongues. He listened carefully and heard the stillness. He detected the murky clamor that desert dwellers have learned to hear in the majestic stillness—the clamor that is always the secret message of stillness, a clamor that diviners call the gibberish of eternity.

He listened carefully for a long time and was about to continue on his way when a nagging whisper stopped him. He paused to listen carefully again. He began to spy on this stillness once more. He tried to discern the whispered temptation in the sound of the stillness, the symbol in the voice of the silence, the worldly disturbance in the gibberish of eternity. He froze and held his breath. He focused his entire body on listening and transformed his limbs into ears. So he heard; he heard another convulsion in the clamor of the ages. He detected a distant, disturbing, monotonous pulse like the songs of grains of sand complaining in the deserts to the gloomy expanses of night about the days' raging heat. Had the quake's hour arrived? Don't scholars say a similar sound precedes earthquakes?

He gazed up again at the horizons, which were partially obscured by the circular wall of the oasis. Then he spotted dust rising in all directions. A bloody circle of red dust particles from the Red Hammada was swirling into the empty air like a whirlwind. Had the attack begun? Had the whirlwind's hour arrived?

He knelt on the dirt and rested his ear on the ground. Then he heard the convulsion even more clearly. Countless nations were advancing. Countless feet were marching his way. The Day of Reckoning had arrived. The armies would storm the walls before evening fell.

He decided he had to act quickly.

He traversed the empty alleys at a brisk pace almost like a canter. He lurched forward till he had left all the buildings behind. Before reaching the fields, he remembered the treasures. He recalled his plan for dealing with the treasures and smiled maliciously. He smirked smugly at the strategy he had devised to conceal the treasures. He smiled because he was sure the invaders would not discover even one of the gold or silver coins. He smiled because he was certain that he had ruined the chances to plunder for armies that had not embarked on this raid and endured the campaign's terrors for any reason except a lust for swag. Yesterday he had spoiled their opportunity to seize the women. Today he had deprived them of the opportunity to lay hold of the treasures. So just when they thought themselves the victors, they would taste defeat, because a warrior who returns from a campaign without any booty is a defeated soldier, even if he has won the battle. This was his present for the leader of the foreigners. This was his gift to the idol. This was the revenge he had prepared for the scarecrow, the ghoul, the dragon. Hee, hee, hee, hee. . . .

He reached the well and waded into the brook barefoot. He trampled carpets of grass underfoot, and the world's ills slipped from his body. His foot plunged into the mire of the field, and the antidote for all the world's ills flowed through his being. The humid breeze, which carried the scent of mud, grasses, and a fig tree, passed over him, and the poisons of chaos were drawn from his soul. He shed his tattered garments one at a time. He pulled off his shorts and tunic. He removed even his veil and stretched out in the mire. He sank into it till he disappeared. Then he poked his nostrils above the surface to take a breath and released a deep moan like the gasp of longing that springs from the chests of ecstatic mystics. He wallowed. He wallowed in the mud to rinse away the pains of angst. He wallowed in the field's muck to cleanse himself of the world's muck. He rolled about in the belly of the earth to free himself from the grasp of deceit. He resumed a journey he had interrupted the day he embraced the beautiful widow and entered the fields with her. He had entered the fields with her because he was certain that once a man enters the fields, he should never leave them. He had suspected that once a man enters cultivated fields, he must become part of the fields: the shadow of a tree, the trunk of a palm, or a plant growing by the brook. He had thought that fields are man's homeland. He had suspected that orchards are man's destiny and his paradise on the day he returns to them, but the beautiful woman had given the lie to his preconceptions and destroyed his certainty. So he had lost his wager, because he had not understood that anyone who makes a bet with a beautiful woman is destined to lose. He had returned from his orchards that day with an unpleasant sense of failure. He had borne in his hands the shackle he had drawn from the comfort of despair, childhood, and forgetfulness. He had waded in the mires of deceit for a long time, and now his circuit was finally leading him to the shores of stillness. Here he was cheek by jowl with the orchard. His body was the mud, his blood was the brook's water, and his hair was the grass of the field. His breath was a breeze freshened by the fragrance of flowers, grass, and damp earth.

He did not know how long this encounter lasted, but when he crept away and entered the nearby skin-clad frame to borrow the scarecrow's body, the field had donned evening's sash.

Hünibach, the Swiss Alps
1998 CE

ABOUT THE AUTHOR

Ibrahim al-Koni, who was born in 1948, is an international author with many authentic, salient identities. He is an award-winning Arabic-language novelist who has already published more than seventy volumes, a Moscow-educated visionary who sees an inevitable interface between myth and contemporary life, an environmentalist, a writer who depicts desert life with great accuracy and emotional depth, a Tuareg whose mother tongue is Tamasheq, and a resident of Switzerland from 1993 through 2012, although he currently lives in Spain. Ibrahim al-Koni, winner of the 2005 Mohamed Zafzaf Award for the Arabic Novel and the 2008 Sheikh Zayed Award for Literature, has also received a Libyan state prize for literature and art, prizes in Switzerland, including the literary prize of the Canton of Bern, and a prize from the Franco-Arab Friendship Committee in 2002 for *L'Oasis cachée*. In 2010, he was awarded the Egyptian State Prize for the Arabic Novel. And in 2015 he was named as one of the ten finalists for the Man Booker International Prize for his body of work.

Al-Koni spent his childhood in the Sahara desert. Then, after working for the Libyan newspapers *Fazzan* and *al-Thawra*, he studied comparative literature at the Maxim Gorky Literature Institute in Moscow, where he later worked as a journalist. He lived in Warsaw for nine years and edited the Polish-language periodical *as-Sadaqa*, which published translations of short stories from Arabic, including some of his own. His novels *The Bleeding of the Stone, Gold Dust, Anubis, The Seven Veils of Seth, New Waw,* and *The Puppet* have been published in English translation, and *The Fetishists* is highly anticipated. At least seven of his titles have appeared in French, and at least ten exist in German translation. Representative works by al-Koni are available in approximately thirty-five languages, including Japanese.

A rare talk by Ibrahim al-Koni (in Arabic with English subtitles) appears at http://channel.louisiana.dk/video/ibrahim-al-koni-desert-we-visit-death, and also on YouTube.

CPSIA information can be obtained at www.ICGtesting.com
Printed in the USA
LVOW10s1132060815

448707LV00011B/60/P

9 781477 302521